RICKIE
TRUJILLO

RICKIE TRUJILLO

NICHOLAS BRADLEY

Lines from *We Never Stopped Crossing Borders* used by permission of Luis J. Rodriguez

For Permissions, contact Upper Hand Press.

Cover and interior design by Stewart A. Williams
This book has been typeset in Adobe Minion.

Upper Hand Press
P. O. Box 91179
Bexley, Ohio 43209
U.S.A.
https://upperhandpress.com

Upper Hand
PRESS

Printed by Bookmasters

ISBN: 978-0-9984906-2-5

FOR AMBER, AUGUSTINE AND ALEXANDER

We were invisible people in a city which thrived on glitter,
big screens and big names, but this glamor contained
none of our names, none of our faces.

The refrain "this is not your country" echoed for a lifetime.

LUIS J. RODRIGUEZ
We Never Stopped Crossing Borders

ACKNOWLEDGMENTS

This book has been a long time in the writing, and consequently I owe thanks to a great many people. Ann Starr of Upper Hand Press, has been an unflagging believer, advisor, and champion of this book from her initial reading of the manuscript. Emily Williamson, content editor, worked with great dedication and care on the manuscript, and the result is infinitely better for her efforts, and she has my deepest gratitude. Andy Koppel was the sharp-eyed copy editor for the manuscript and found those little and not so little problems with the text. I am so grateful for his ability to see what I could not. Thanks, as well, to Peg Keller for her friendship, guidance, and advice for more years than either one of us cares to remember.

I am indebted to my teachers, beginning with Carl Hartman at Michigan State and David Anderson at California State University, Northridge. I am also indebted to Stephen Rivele for reading and critiquing an early version of the manuscript.

A number of people read drafts of the manuscript and offered insight and advice, for which I am profoundly grateful: Thompson Bradley read each sentence, paragraph and page with great care and offered up suggestions that were invaluable; Robert Oppenheim, Mildene Bradley, and Edward Bradley did the same. Others read the manuscript with an eye for authenticity:

I turned often to Diego Duarte, Blanca Guzman, and, early on, Hector Ramirez, to check on the correct Spanish or facts about the neighborhood or the immigrant experience in general. Los Angeles School Police Sergeant Danny Arambulo and Probation Officer Juan Casteñeda offered their knowledge and support as well. With care and compassion each person pointed out areas that needed to be addressed to make the book stronger, and areas of strength, which gave me hope.

There is a long list of people who offered much needed and appreciated words of encouragement and support: Donald Bradley, Jr., O.T. Bradley, Juliet Radhayrapetian, Shant Amirian, Med Flory, Sherman Ferguson, Anni Wall, Nancy Franyutti, Anjli Kohli, Vern Vaden, Antonio Reveles, among many more. Thank you.

Thank you to the personnel at North Hollywood High School for being so accommodating: Ricardo Rosales, Principal; Carrie Schwartz, Assistant Principal; Linda Szabo, Aracely Jovel, Ruby Castillo; Maria Lopez; Markuz Velasquez; Kenneth Harris, and Andrew Lepore.

A special thanks to James Trujillo for his help in guiding me through the world of social media: I am so grateful for your patience and expertise.

No writer could ask for a finer group of friends and advisors.

RICKIE TRUJILLO

CHAPTER 1

Rickie Trujillo stands on the edge of the wide patio and the steps down to the sidewalk at the entrance to the high school. He lets others flow around him as if he were a boulder in a stream. Students gather in groups on the patio, on the steps and on the sidewalk with loud talk and laughter and shouting.

Friday. The school day is over, the weekend is here and Rickie can finally breathe easy. He looks around for other members of his crew, Alex particularly, but then he remembers that Alex had to take his mom to the clinic.

Tony? Dennis? They're both in Special Education classes. Rickie doesn't have class with either of them. They spend a lot of time in the Deans' Office because they fool around in class and ditch often. He wonders if they're with one of the deans now. Rickie looks around for Wagner or his partner; he knows Wagner is going to be pissed that Rickie left the office earlier without his permission, but so what? Rickie doesn't find him or the female dean in the crowd of people at the entrance.

Oscar? Rickie doesn't know where he is, and he doesn't care. Oscar's a new student from Pacoima. Rickie said it was okay for Oscar to join their crew before he knew anything about him, but now he regrets it. Oscar's a braggart and a liar, and worst of all, a bully. He says he and some friends almost kicked a kid to death and took part in a gang rape. He's probably full of shit, but he's going to be a problem for Rickie because Rickie feels challenged by him. Rickie will have to do something to prove himself again to the others if he doesn't want Oscar to take over the crew.

He looks around for Claudia but doesn't find her, either; her mom has probably already picked her up. They have been boyfriend and girlfriend for a few months, but her parents keep a close watch on her; she doesn't leave the house except for school or in the company of her mother. She has a woman's body, but is still a little kid sometimes; she laughs loudly about silly shit and cries easily. Rickie doesn't really know what he feels about her. They have never done much of anything. He goes to her house sometimes and sits on the sofa with her to watch TV, and they make out quietly. Her mother stays in the kitchen and listens, but she doesn't come unannounced into the living room; she keeps Claudia's younger sisters out, too.

Rickie enjoys the shade of the overhanging oaks at the top of the steps. He listens to groups of students make plans for the weekend or tell a parent on a cellphone where to pick them up, but he himself has no place to go in a hurry. He looks over the people standing on the sidewalk at the bottom of the steps and catches the eye of the principal, Jim Garcia. Rickie has not had to deal with him, has never even spoken to him, but he sees the man appraising him now. He notices Rickie's Taz shirt and tries to read his face and his stance. Is he a troublemaker or a reformed troublemaker? Is the man supposed to be wary of the boy, keep an eye on him? It is clear he doesn't know the answers to these questions. But on Monday, when the principal hears from Maltrey and Wagner, he'll know who Rickie is.

Rickie was late getting up this morning. Very late. He wakes up in a sweat. He sleeps with the window locked and the shade and the curtains drawn, and the room heats up quickly on these late spring mornings. In this neighborhood, people don't leave ground floor windows open, even with wrought iron bars at the windows. An open window is an invitation, and Rickie's grandmother doesn't have the money to secure the windows. They do have a heavy black security door at the front, installed by Rickie's brother and his friends. They say they got it at the swap meet.

Rickie takes a long hot shower in an attempt to clear his head, but it still feels achy and thick with sleep. He debates not going to school at all, but being home inside would be worse than boring. Instead, he decides to take his time getting to school. He doesn't catch the bus, opting to walk the distance. By the time he gets near the school, lunch is over and the fifth period of the day is underway. When the school cops approach, Rickie is standing outside the 7-Eleven wishing he had some money for something to eat. The cops pull into the 7-Eleven parking lot, give the siren a short whoop, and command Rickie to raise his hands and turn to put them on the hood of the car. They recognize him as truant and as a tagger, and they put him in handcuffs to take him to school.

The school police officers park in front and escort Rickie into the school. The school is old and ignored, and there are no metal detectors at the entrance, so the officers sign him in at a small table by the front door, manned by an older parent volunteer who proudly wears an orange shirt identifying him as security. One of the officers has Rickie by the elbow.

"We're taking him to the Deans' Office," he says. The parent volunteer nods; these two officers are at the school often.

Rickie has dark eyes and a shaved head. He is slight, wiry, and shorter than the men on either side of him. He has a wary, hunted expression about the eyes. This is not Rickie's first time being escorted into the school in handcuffs, standard procedure for truants when they're brought into the school.

Wagner, the dean with blond hair and freckles, comes out from his office down the corridor at that moment and sees them coming.

"Rickie, Rickie, Rickie," he calls from the hallway, shaking his head in exaggerated disappointment; Rickie knows the man doesn't really care.

Rickie eyes Wagner disdainfully, tilting his head to the side, then dropping his eyes slowly. He dislikes Wagner and his sarcastic attitude, but he says nothing.

"Truant?" Wagner asks the cops.

"He was hanging out in front of the 7-Eleven."

Wagner turns back to Rickie. "Where were you for periods one through four?"

Rickie doesn't look up. "Home," he says. "I got up late."

"Well, gentlemen," Wagner says, addressing the officers, "Take him to Ruby Lopez, his P.O. Remember? He and his buddy Alex Hernandez got caught joyriding in a 'borrowed' car up in the canyon. You owe Ms. Ramirez and me, Rickie my man; we didn't give you up to the homie who came looking for you. You're still in one piece, so I guess he hasn't found you yet."

Wagner pauses and peers at Rickie, shaking his head back and forth, almost imperceptibly; the man has given up on him. "You're not making life any easier for yourself, bud. Time to grow up." Rickie continues to look down. "I just remembered," Wagner says, turning to the police officers, "Lopez isn't here today. Sit him in here. I wish someone else, *anyone else*, had decided to come to work today!"

They take the handcuffs off and hand the paperwork to the dean before they leave. Rickie sits at a student desk against the wall, his arms folded, watching. Wagner goes into his inner office but in a minute comes out again.

"Did you sign in? No? Sign in on the clipboard. I'll be right back. Sit here until the end of fifth period."

Rickie says nothing and makes no move to sign in. He listens to the dean cross the hall, unlock the faculty men's room door, and lock it behind him. Rickie stands and goes to the office doorway, checks left and right, and walks quietly across the deserted corridor and up the staircase. Maltrey's room is on the second floor; he doesn't teach this period, but he's probably in the room. Claudia goes there during her free period to work at one of the computers. Rickie knows Wagner won't come looking for him.

"I've been teaching for thirty years, and you students have finally worn me out," Maltrey told Rickie's class a few weeks back. Rickie thinks he said it to every class. "You don't do your homework, you're not prepared, you're disrespectful, and you don't care." Rickie almost feels sorry for the old man with his shiny bald head and his thin strands of hair greased in place across the top. Rickie himself is good at math; he doesn't do his homework, but he doesn't usually cause problems for Maltrey or any teacher.

Everybody knows that Maltrey has more than coffee in the thermos he brings to school each day and locks in a filing cabinet. He used to love to teach, he tells the students, but he's grown tired of teaching basic Algebra year after year and has grown exasperated by students giving the same wrong answers and asking the same dumb questions that reveal ignorance of basic arithmetic. But he's particularly worn down by their disruptive behavior. Whatever he puts in that thermos eases him through the day.

"What are you doing here, Rickie?" Maltrey says when Rickie opens the door and walks into the room without asking.

"I want to work on my math," he says as he enters. He doesn't look at Maltrey.

"You aren't having any problems with math."

Rickie doesn't respond. Rather than go to a computer station, he goes right to Claudia, who is staring hard at the screen. He perches on a table in back of her.

"What are you doing?" he asks her.

"Algebra, what else? I don't get this one," she says, pointing at the screen.

Rickie leans in. "Okay. You have to add negative twenty-two to both sides and solve for X. The answer is negative fifteen." As he leans in, he lets his hand rest on her shoulder and then finger walk down toward her breast.

"Rickie!" she says and laughs, louder than she intended. Maltrey comes to stand next to him.

"Rickie, if you're going to be here, take a seat. Don't bother Claudia."

"He's helping..."

Rickie ignores Maltrey.

"Rickie! Do you hear me?"

Rickie continues to ignore the teacher. He sits motionlessly, staring at Claudia's back. He's still angry about Wagner's dismissive attitude toward him. "Shut the hell up," he says quietly, but Maltrey doesn't hear him.

"You can't come in here and bother students who are working. It's time for you to go to your fifth period class." Rickie doesn't move.

"Rickie, look at me. Time to leave." When Rickie makes no move to get up, Maltrey reaches over to turn Rickie's head to face him.

Everyone knows teachers can't put their hands on a kid. Students know it as well as teachers; Rickie knows it. He has seen teachers and students, their faces inches apart, yelling, spit flying, rage suffusing the teacher's face in a violet bloom as he or she holds back a hand longing to strike. If the teacher follows through, he'll get pulled from the classroom and be forced to sit for months in an empty office away from the school. Sometimes parents file charges.

Maltrey disregards what he knows not to do and puts his large hand on the top of Rickie's head to turn it to face him. He no longer has the patience to be ignored.

It surprises Rickie. He turns and catches a glimpse of the teacher's face before his own rage takes over. He sees anger there, but something else as well in the heavy eyes and sagging jow—sadness, a loss of hope, the inevitability of failure. Rickie experiences a flash of pity for the old man that instantaneously disappears.

"Hey, motherfucker, don't! Don't touch my head!" He turns

to duck out of Maltrey's grasp.

The teacher adjusts his grip, but does not let go. His hand is big and strong. "Turn! Look at me!"

"Fuck you! That hurts!" He howls loudly for the dramatic effect; other students have turned to watch.

Rickie stands and sharply jerks his head out of Maltrey's grip. The teacher puts his arm out to stop the boy from leaving the classroom, but he pushes by it.

"Rickie! Come back here! Come back here right now!"

At the doorway, Rickie turns to face the teacher. "You hurt me," he says. "Watch! You're going to pay... I'm going to fuck you up," he yells and then slams the door open. The bell rings at that moment, loud and insistent. The boy immediately blends in with the crowd of students emptying out of classrooms into the corridor and heading for their last class of the day. He hesitates: leave campus or go to Phelan's English class? He knows that even though Maltrey put his hands on him, he will get in trouble for threatening the old man; Maltrey will report what happened, and Rickie will be moved out of the school at least. Since he's on probation, it might even be worse. But it won't happen today; he smelled the alcohol on Maltrey's breath. Maltrey will wait until early Monday morning. And who cares anyway if security comes and takes him out of Phelan's class? Rickie will just take off, and they won't follow.

Rickie enters quietly by the back door and takes his seat in Bill Phelan's sixth period English class; he's the only student in a last row of three desks. He doesn't have anyone to talk with because Phelan moved the one kid who used to sit back there with him. It doesn't bother Rickie; he sits quietly and doesn't do anything.

Phelan encourages Rickie, but he doesn't harp on him. Only once, early on, Phelan called Rickie's grandmother because he wasn't doing his work.

"My grandma doesn't really understand English," Rickie said the next day. "She didn't understand your Spanish, either, but she thought you sounded nice."

The classroom is dark and cool. A sentence correction warm-up is on the screen at the front of the room. Rickie actually gets up and borrows a piece of paper and makes a half-hearted attempt to do the work, but he is preoccupied by his confrontation with Maltrey; he glances at the doorway every time someone enters. Rickie turns his paper over and practices his tag, "Grt Whyt." Phelan moves around the classroom checking the students' work. He approaches Rickie, who turns the paper over to the front.

"Why aren't you finished with the first one?" Phelan asks. He looks at Rickie with pale blue eyes.

"I can't see it."

"Move up closer."

"Naw, I'm good. I'll copy it from Veronica."

"That's not the point," Phelan says. He shakes his head.

"I know, Phelan. Chill, dude. I'm just messin' with you. I'll give it a try."

Phelan looks at him for a long moment; he doesn't push harder.

"What?"

"I know you can do this stuff. Or used to be able to before you gave up."

"I'll start now," Rickie says with a smile.

"Where have I heard that before?"

"I will. You'll see. I'm going to get an A in this class."

"It won't happen by wishing for it, you know."

The teacher checks the class. Most are still busy doing the warm-up. The dim light and the cool air seem to keep everyone calm and working, even though it's the last period of the day on Friday.

"C'mon. Try, Rickie. It won't kill you."

When the teacher turns to work with other students, Rickie goes back to practicing his tag on the clean sheet of paper he's borrowed. He is barely aware of the class going over the warm-up.

Why didn't he just stand up and go to a computer? Why did he have to fight with Maltrey? He's a good old guy, patient and slow. Some students even kid him—"Hey, Mr. Maltrey, what've we got in that thermos today? Margaritas? Rum and Coke? Ah, I know—Mexican coffee," some smartass will call out—but Maltrey still teaches, even if he's in a haze. Rickie likes him. Rickie knows that he, not Maltrey, is the problem.

He looks up and watches Phelan, who is leaning in as other students read their corrections aloud to one another. Rickie pays attention with half an ear. He likes watching others when they aren't aware they're being watched; likes being able to view everything at a distance as though through a telescope, detached like that, though still able to see clearly. It makes him feel somehow untouchable, powerful. He can't remember when he started doing this, but he thinks it was when he was a little boy witnessing his parents fight, or if not witnessing, then listening to them when they were out of sight. He remembers lying in bed and pretending that the bed was a boat that he had set sail in. He would gather the covers about him and hold them close so that only his head was exposed. As long as he was in this bed, in this boat, he could sail safely and warmly across the stormy sea. When he imagined it well enough, he drifted through the voices that rose like the wind and the lashing spray of words and the slamming doors into peaceful sleep.

He likes this feeling best of all, this detachment from everything: the silence, the inner stillness.

CHAPTER 2

Rickie continues to enjoy the cool shade of the oak trees, reluctant to move. The principal has looked away now and is talking with a group of skate boarders. It gives Rickie a chance to envision what will happen on Monday.

He'll have to see his Probation Officer, Ms. Lopez. Maltrey won't let it go; he'll report the incident to the principal. Then Garcia will know who Rickie is. There will be a meeting of school police, the principal, Maltrey, Wagner, Lopez, and Rickie's grandmother—Lopez will translate for her. Maltrey will write up that Rickie was defiant and threatened him. They will kick Rickie out and he'll end up in another school at least. Maybe worse.

Lopez will stick up for him at that meeting. She's good. Rickie's in one of her counseling groups with other kids on probation. When she asks questions, she listens to the answers. She sits quietly and actually hears the outrage from the boys like Mauricio who had to be removed from the house after he'd been beaten by his mother's boyfriend; or like Ernesto who was jumped by a gang of punks in the park, who took his new phone that he can't afford to replace. Lopez hears the aching and almost wordless pain of those kids who are ignored, who are so unimportant that they're all but invisible shadows at home and at school, who sit off by themselves as though they're ashamed of taking up space. Lopez learns their names and makes them come into the circle. She knows how dangerous the isolated ones are.

Lopez has been to Rickie's house to talk with his grandmother, who tells the officer about Rickie's parents and his grandfather. Lopez has been inside apartments crowded with two or three families and garages turned into makeshift living quarters; she knows about the fathers who stand on corners to offer themselves as day-laborers and the mothers who work as domestics; about the black kids who live in group homes or in the shelter with large, worn out mothers; about the white kids who live in leaky trailers with impossibly skinny and short-tempered mothers and their violent boyfriends. She knows who's talking shit to whom, who's going to get her ass kicked, who's been jumped, who's been flashed or propositioned by some pervert in a van with his hard-on in his hand. She's from East L.A., and she's tough.

"I don't have time for your bullshit," she tells her clients. "You be honest with me, and I'll be honest with you." She doesn't let a dean or a cop or the principal dismiss a kid without reminding them of the truths about life in this neighborhood.

Lopez and others encourage Rickie to express his feelings, but people don't realize that the only feeling he can easily identify is the red anger that sometimes overtakes him. Anger: at his father and his mother for deserting his brother and sister and him; at God for allowing his grandfather to die; at his grandmother for still attending church and worshipping that God; at teachers and other adults who don't see him or hear him and only want him to do what they want him to do; and at punks who think they can bully him. This anger is too big and terrifying to let take form in his body, like a bad genie in a black and red and roiling cloud that will overwhelm him. They don't realize, people like Lopez, the danger in allowing that thing to come to life.

But Lopez will be on his side; she'll try to keep him at the school so that she can monitor him. He knows she likes him, sees something worth saving that others don't; she even told him that he has a nice smile that makes him handsome. But this time she'll lose; he knows he has crossed the line.

CHAPTER 3

The front steps and the wide entrance to the school have emptied. Only a few students remain in conversation with Jim Garcia out at the sidewalk. When they leave, the principal will mount the steps and maybe want to speak with Rickie. He doesn't want that, doesn't want to be known yet. Rickie walks slowly down the steps, past this remaining group, and crosses the street. He heads for the bus stop, relieved to remember again that it's Friday. Monday is a weekend away.

He walks east past the elementary school playground on the north side of the street and the 7-Eleven across from it, where he recognizes a few kids from class buying chili cheese dogs and chips and sodas. He doesn't have any money on him, hasn't eaten all day in fact, because he didn't ask for money from his grandmother this morning. He doesn't some mornings. He knows they live close to the edge. If he wants money, he needs to get a job. After baseball season, maybe.

He scans the people in 7-Eleven to see if he knows any of them well enough to mooch some chips or a bite of hotdog from one of them. He doesn't. He walks on by, past an office building with scaffolding to the second story that he and Alex, Dennis and Tony climbed the past Saturday night, late. They peered down into the restaurant open 24/7 across the street to see what people do late at night who aren't tagging or partying. The customers they could see sat alone or in tired, unspeaking couples. Rickie wanted to be there, too, served by a waitress who called you "Sweetie" and who brought you coffee and a sandwich in this restaurant casting its warm light out onto the sidewalk of an otherwise dark and deserted street.

The boys tagged the windows and the bare sandstone of the building. Rickie looks up—there it is, his tag, "Grt Whyt," in simple angular black letters. Not a bomb—no color, no clownish bubble letters, no art like the work he has seen on the concrete sides of the L.A. River or on the walls along the 10 freeway in East L.A.—just sharp, angry angles that remind him of shark's teeth. Strong. A claim, a reclamation of the neighborhood, not only from other tagging crews, but from the white people as well who own this building and think they can clean it up and take it from the neighborhood. He has taken it back. No one has dared to cross him out; no one has buffed his tag.

He stands at the bus stop next to Starbucks. A homeless man wearing a wool cap, fingerless gloves and a dirty coat even in this heat, pushes a shopping cart filled with matted brown blankets and plastic grocery bags stuffed with unidentifiable junk onto the sidewalk and waits for patrons to come out of the coffee shop. Most ignore him. A few give him some coins, which he inspects dismally after they pass by. Rickie looks into his sad, bloodshot eyes, and shrugs his shoulders—no money.

By the time the bus comes, a few more kids from the high school have joined Rickie. He gets on, shows his pass, and goes to the back. The other kids sit in the front. The bus driver checks Rickie, recognizes him as a tagger, and keeps him in the mirror. When the bus arrives at his stop, Rickie waits for a boy and girl to get off. They ride the same route each day, going and coming, but they never exchange more than a nod or a Hi. Long ago he sized them up as good students, whose mothers, or mothers and fathers, will move them out of the neighborhood to some place like Santa Clarita as soon as they have enough money. These kids go home to someone waiting for them. And even if there is no one, the place will feel as though someone is going to be back soon. They go home, have a snack, sleep until dinner, help clean up, do their homework, take a shower and go to bed. Rickie has heard them talk about life at home, so safe, so assured. On the weekends, they help with the housework and do the weekend's homework. Maybe someone plays soccer or softball. Otherwise, they stay inside most of the time to watch TV and play video games, or they go to the park as a family. Trouble doesn't follow them and it won't find them. It finds people like Rickie.

CHAPTER 4

The heat throbs. For the past week, it has given weight to each day as soon as the sun rises, seems to engulf trees and the poor cinderblock houses, desiccate grass and shrubs, bake cars parked on the streets or in driveways until they pulse with hot, close air. Paint peels. Wood dries and splinters. Metal sears unsuspecting fingers. The air smells only of dust and dry things—a flat, funereal scent.

Rickie gets off the bus ahead of the boy and girl, who stand still for a moment, dumbstruck by the heat but also waiting for Rickie to get ahead of them. He crosses the street and walks the uneven sidewalk alone and in silence, merging with the heat and the baked landscape.

His face does not register much thought or emotion, just the self-absorption of his seventeen years. His eyes, however, are active, not to understand the landscape he sees in front of him, but seeking information he will need to process quickly; he needs to be wary and aware in this neighborhood of drive-bys and car-loads of *vatos locos* who jump out and nearly beat you to death before they jump back in the car and scream off laughing. He can't afford to be surprised.

He walks, not seeing the details of the neighborhood he walks through. As far as he knows, things have always been as they are now; they have a weight and a past. He doesn't understand the importance of this neighborhood of small post-war houses, old now and many in need of repair, or take in the occasional brave lawn, the usual dirt front yards, the open windows with curtains tied in a knot to allow the passage of air. He doesn't notice the shirtless men and the women in poor dresses sitting with their heads down, hands clasped between their legs under shade trees in back yards with broken appliances or milk crates pushed off to the side; with maybe an abandoned car which little ones pretend to drive; perhaps a chicken or two pecking in the clumps of grass; or a garden plot with small plants of green or red *chiles* standing in moist and darkened mounds. Or, if he sees these things at all, they signify nothing, even though his grandfather had explained their importance.

Abuelo told Rickie—whom his grandparents and brother and sister call Junior—about these streets and neighborhoods, things that Rickie only imperfectly understood. They drove in his grandfather's pick-up truck one Sunday morning. The man pointed out windows open on the second story of large block apartment buildings and the foil on the west and south-facing windows to reflect away the sun's heat, and he told how the people in these buildings were like them and didn't have air-conditioning or couldn't afford to run it. He told Rickie that the materials used to build these places were cheap; that's why boards warped and doors didn't hang correctly, and paint faded and peeled or turned to chalk so quickly. If he lived in one of these apartment buildings, his grandfather said with a laugh, he would always worry about electrical fires because he knew about the cheap wiring and fixtures that barely met code. He had put some of it in himself, he said, and then he laughed again.

It made no difference how careless the workmanship in these places or how small and old the houses seemed now, he said. This neighborhood represented a huge step on a journey that had begun with a driving ambition and desperate need; that had led to long dusty walks, running, hiding in stinking culverts, resting in the shade of boulders, surviving in shacks that were little more than sticks and pieces of cardboard in makeshift camps reeking of dirty diapers and rotting fruit; that had meant taking a chance on harrowing night journeys in the backs of trucks, hidden behind and under who knew what, always with a fear of vicious dogs and men, some in uniform on both sides of the border, who counted lives and a person's few possessions as nothing and would dispose of either with cold, disparaging eyes.

He and his grandfather sat in the parked truck in the lot of Home Depot, the old man smelling warmly of tortillas and coffee and the sweat of work clothes, and the man told the boy that along with one crossing, another crossing took place, one you had not accounted for, were not warned about: You had entered a country that was a no-place, an indifferent landscape where you would remain anonymous and tolerated only so long as you rode the early morning or late evening buses and quietly took care of the homes and children of the rich, swept darkened hallways and backrooms, mopped bathrooms, vacuumed thick carpets at night as though you were a ghost, and lived in the neighborhoods others had abandoned.

"Everything around us," the old man said with the door of the pick-up open, ready to move on into the store, "this neighborhood, which is the only world you know, and the police who patrol it and the churches which draw from its people and the schools which educate you and all the other children... This neighborhood tells us that this is not home. It wants us to move on or go back to our home country. But then it wants us to stay here, too, to do the backbreaking work no one else will do. These people don't know what they want.

"But we stay, *mi'jo*, even though we are sometimes alone and sometimes in fear, and we do good work, in spite of everything, and we survive," and the old man laughed and got out of the truck.

The shades are pulled and the drapes drawn, but the hot stillness has entered his grandmother's small house. He closes the front door behind him. Slants of sunlight come in at the window and cut across the kitchen floor into this room, showing the worn and dirty armrests of the sofa, the dark blanket that covers the cushions, the mismatched tables and lamps, the shabby glider that someone gave them. Everything is nearly used up. Except for the TV. She has left it on, *abuelita*, as she often does. She says she likes to have the beautiful men and women of the *novelas* and the handsome newsreaders there in her living room, even if she's not there. The thought of them in her house comforts her, particularly while she is away cleaning other people's houses in different parts of the city. These people protect her *casita* as well. She believes that they somehow care about her and will not let anything bad happen to her house while she is away. Her grandchildren cannot convince her otherwise.

She wanted a nice TV to house her television friends, she said, so she bought this large one and the dark wooden cabinet to hold it. It is her pride. She polishes the wood daily, dusts the screen, sits in the evenings with her hands folded in delight and laughs at the comedians and admires the voices of the beautiful singers so lavishly attired.

Rickie punches the button to turn the TV off and listens in the silence for the whirr of the fan next to it that usually sends a welcome breeze toward the sofa. It's off. He thinks about turning it on and sitting on the sofa to cool off, but he doesn't. He walks into the kitchen instead, rummages in the fridge until he finds some pizza left over from mid-week, and eats it as he stands in the cold air from the open refrigerator door.

Two more weeks of school. Baseball playoffs tomorrow and the championship next weekend if they win. Then summer. He'll have to get a job; his brother will insist on it, but he doesn't want to. Rickie hopes that his arrest will make getting a job difficult. He really wants to stay home and sit in front of the fan, or kick it with his homies at their houses.

Some worry presses in on him, a dark necessity looming in the distance, but what is it? He should know what it is, but he can't bring it to mind. He doesn't want to know it.

He reaches for a soda. *Abuelita* would yell at him for standing with the refrigerator door open like this.

Rickie goes into his bedroom. His whole world is here, everything he cares about. On top of a crocheted blanket his grandmother has folded on his dresser, there is a sort of shrine to his baseball playing. Team photos, many trophies, a photo of himself as MVP on the cover of a phony Sports Illustrated taken at Knotts Berry Farm, and his all-star caps from the past years.

The trophies are reflected in the mirror in back of the dresser, doubling their number. He is the sole occupant of his own Hall of Fame. He used to envision what this dresser would look like by the end of high school. His older brother, Bill, told him he would buy a glass case in which to store his trophies, and they had laughed about how big it would be.

"We'll have to move you out of your room, *abuelita*, to put all of Junior's trophies. What will you do when the newspaper reporters come to interview you about your major league grandson?" Bill asked her in Spanish.

She shook her head. "I don't care about baseball," she said.

These days Rickie doesn't look at his trophies much. He used to wipe them down each week, but now they gather dust until his grandmother notices and cleans the top of his dresser. He doesn't think about his future in baseball very often any more either. He used to see himself starring in high school, being scouted, signed, playing minor league ball in a town somewhere in the San Joaquin Valley or some place in the South, riding buses from game to game, finally getting his chance to go to "the Show." That's what they called it in a movie he's seen. He wonders if they really do.

It isn't as though he suddenly hates baseball. He still plays in a game every Wednesday and Saturday, practices Tuesday, Thursday and Friday. But the game has lost its luster. Baseball is no longer the sure avenue to the future it once seemed to be. He doesn't know when the change took place. One day he became aware of feeling a desperate aloneness. He began to worry that he was going to die before he reached twenty. Lopez told the group that most kids feel these fears as they enter adolescence, but rather than ease the fear, her easy dismissiveness made Rickie angry.

He wanted to shout to the world that he no longer cared about baseball or his trophies or his Xbox or the baseball and basketball cards he had so carefully preserved in plastic sheets inside large three-ring binders or Taz or anything that he had once thought important.

Life has lost dimension, has no depth or length or width, has simply become one day followed by another that amounts to nothing, like steps taken across an expanse of desert, one footstep in the sand looking exactly like the next, going nowhere, perhaps only in a circle. He wants to scream his fear about this to someone, but to whom? Lopez? Maybe. A teacher? A counselor? He snorts at those ideas. Teachers are all too wrapped up in their grades and lessons. Counselors never counsel. They have too many papers to sign, papers to sort, papers to file.

Who then? His brother? His sister? They're too busy working. When they aren't, Bill goes to parties and Daisy goes to school all the time. He wonders about them. Maybe they feel the same disconnectedness he does, and that's why they go to school and parties and work, just to cover the emptiness where purpose and belief and happiness are supposed to be.

A TV stands on a bookshelf next to his dresser. The bookshelf has no books in it, but there are a few Xbox games, some DVDs, and some magazines, *Low Riders* and a few old issues of *Mad* and *SI*. His Xbox gathers dust on top of the TV.

Rickie hardly watches TV, but he lies back on the bed and turns it on with the remote as though to discover why it holds so little interest for him. He turns to a cartoon channel—little kids' stuff. ESPN—car racing, two men talking about some upcoming race. MTV—girls in bikinis on a beach, one blonde, one dark, both with beautiful lips, full, round breasts barely covered by little triangles of cloth. They are jabbering about something and laughing. Who cares? Maybe they think they're saying something important or funny, but they're pathetic. He and every other boy knows why they're there. He glances at the clock. Practice in twenty minutes. Ten minutes to walk to the park. He has time. Just him in the house. He reaches down and undoes his belt.

Normally he thinks about someone he knows, but not too well. Never the girls at school even though some of them, like Gloria, are hot. Not Claudia. They're too close, too known. It has to be an adult, someone young, a little distant but who clearly knows things. Like the young woman next door who says hi to him, whose nurse's uniforms are tight across the hips and breasts. Or some young female teacher who might wear a skirt a little too short and sit facing him with her legs open just enough or a blouse too loose, who might thoughtlessly or, even better, on purpose, lean over to work with another student and reveal the rounded globes of her breasts, then look up and catch him and smile knowingly. Women who know, who touch him, pet him, caress him, who kiss him passionately but with tearful, sympathetic eyes, who want him in a way they never want boyfriends or husbands, who find ways for the two of them to be alone--in a darkened classroom, in the back seat of a car, here in this room, the women sneaking in and out of the window, feverish to get to him because only he can quiet their moaning, their clutching hands, their bodies writhing beneath him or swooping and diving on top of him; only he can bring them to hissing, grunting, high-arching, wild-eyed release.

As he cleans himself, he becomes aware of the noise and jumble of images issuing from the TV depicting teenagers playing sports on the beach or driving, everybody beautiful and rich enough to spend their time doing nothing but this, against the background of a song he doesn't recognize but he's sure is a song by a rock band that white kids listen to. He clicks the TV off and silence fills the room. He lies on the bed without moving. He experiences the emptiness he always feels afterwards. Now that release has come, he plumbs the depths of his need and feels the absence of tenderness and mother-loving. That's what he misses. When he and a girl finally do it, Claudia probably, he fears that he will feel just like this. Will he search her face and not know her?

CHAPTER 5

Rickie shows up for practice about a minute before it begins. "I don't know why," he says when his coach gently chides him about being the last one there, the first one gone.

"You used to be the first one here and didn't leave until it was dark. What happened?"

"I don't like hanging around."

"*Mi'jo*, with your skills... A little extra practice around the bag, a little more hitting... This is the time to put in the extra effort."

"I'll try next practice, Coach," Rickie says, but they both know he won't be there early.

Rickie takes batting practice. He never tries to hit for power. He is short and thin, delicate for a seventeen-year-old. Occasionally someone in the past felt safe calling him *puto* or *maricón* because of his small stature, but they didn't know about the anger he wore below the surface like a fiery undergarment. One time, when he was in eighth grade, Rickie went after a kid more than twice his size. They were out on the field at P.E. A group of boys was choosing up sides and positions for flag football. Rickie told a big kid that he was too slow to be quarterback.

"Hey, *maricón*, suck my dick," the kid said to him.

They were standing in a group waiting for the teacher to come out from the gym office with the flags, belts and football; the teachers always took their time getting out to the field.

The big kid's friend knew about Rickie. "What do you want to say that for, fool? You *are* too slow. You should block."

"Shut up."

Rickie didn't wait. He charged the kid and knocked him down. When he was on top of him, he began to hit him as hard as he could in the face. When the kid was bleeding from his mouth and nose, Rickie seemed to grow more dangerous and detached. The big kid howled and held Rickie's hands away with fearful desperation. The others dragged Rickie off, and Alex held him in a bear hug until the rage passed. By the time the teacher got there, everything was over. The big kid said he'd been tackled hard and hit his face. The teacher looked at the other boys, and they all concurred. The teacher shrugged and sent him to the nurse.

"Let's play *flag* football, guys, okay? No more rough stuff," the teacher said.

From that day on they called Rickie "the shark" or Jaws; a boy who witnessed this attack said that Rickie's eyes looked like a shark's eyes during a feeding frenzy. The name stuck, but only a few referred to it openly. Rickie was proud of his reputation; that's when he adopted his tag, "Grt Whyt." The big boy, Alberto, and all of his friends who had been there or heard about it later, were sure that Rickie was crazy and would kill someone one day. He and his friends kept their distance from Rickie and didn't make eye contact with him when they passed him in the hallway.

Rickie performs with a liquid grace at second base that sometimes surprises even him; when someone asks him about it, he says he sees everything that's about to happen before it does. He occasionally catches Coach Vega marveling at his talent: he has agility, speed, a great glove, and intelligence in the field and at the plate. He can hit the curve and the fastball, can lay down a bunt, take a pitch when called upon, or hit behind the runner in a hit and run. He can turn a double play smoothly. Rickie shines with pride when he knows he is playing well and the coach is watching.

He's been there, too, in a nearby booth with other teammates, when the coaches talk about players at their Saturday morning meetings at Denny's; when they compare notes, laugh about some players, speak with a kind of reverence about others. After a while, the coaches forget that players are in booths within hearing distance.

"That kid, your second baseman, he's got skills."

"Skills? Just skills? The kid is amazing."

"Are you just realizing that, man? The kid's been playing like that for years."

"Did you see him against us?" another coach joins in. Most of the coaches are at the fields for one another's games. "Damn! We've got runners at first and third, no outs. The batter, you know, Sammy, hits a hard grounder over second. Your kid, I don't know how, he gets there, backhands it, holds the runner at third, flips an easy throw behind his back to the shortstop who throws on to first for a double play. I thought I was watching the damn Dodgers for a moment. The next kid strikes out and we lose the game by a run. Your kid has got baseball sense, *compa*. He knows the game like from birth. You want to trade him?"

"Yeah, for your centerfielder who lost his pants chasing the ball to the fence?"

"*Mi cinto se rompio!*" the coach says, making a sad clown face and whining. "I found a piece of rope in the bag and belted his lardass up good!"

Everyone laughs. They played ball in high school and at the local junior colleges together. After they joined the workforce, they formed a park league and coached.

"Or how about mine? Fernando," one of the others joins in. "His *jefita* makes tamales last Friday night. I've had her tamales--"

The others seated around the booth let out a chorus of "Ooohs" and "Aaahs," raise their eyebrows, elbow each other and laugh.

"I've heard about her tamales."

"What did Cynthia say when you told her that you were eating another *vieja's* tamales?"

"No, man, Cynthia was there. It was the team picnic. *Pinches cabrones!* What do you take me for?" he asks and everyone laughs again. "Anyway, she makes them *real* hot, man, and the kid pigs out. Game time Saturday, the kid's in the Andy Gump. He's supposed to catch. 'Fernando, *que pasa*? Are you sick?' I call at the door. He's in there moaning. 'Oh, man, I've got the cold sweats. I'm sick.' He moans again like a bull, man, and I hear that awful sound, you know, *chorro*. 'Fernando, how's your *culo*? Did you eat too many *chiles*?' I'm laughing now. 'Tamales. Don't laugh, Coach, I think I'm going to die. It burns! I'm never going to eat again.' The kid spends the whole game going back and forth to the Andy Gump. He's green, man, sweat all over his forehead, and on a hot day, he's cold. And we lose the game, too. Our power hitter spends the whole time in the Andy Gump!" Rickie and the other boys sitting in the booth with him snicker at this, and Coach Vega raises his eyebrows at them; they look down at their sodas.

The coach across from Miguel Vega asks quietly, "Did your kid, what's his name? Rickie? Did he play ball at school this season?" Rickie strains to hear.

"No. Bad grades. He got in trouble with the law." The coach lowers his voice, glances over at Rickie, who pretends to listen to a joke a teammate is telling. "He got caught with a car. I don't know. He doesn't talk. He's like a ghost. The kids, the other players, they respect him, but he's not real close to any of them. He comes to the field alone, leaves alone. Most of the time. Sometimes there's this other kid, tall, real dark, *moreno*, real quiet, who sits in the stands. Looks like a gangster with his Dickies and long T-shirts. Never causes any problems. When he's there, they leave together. But that's all."

"Any family ever show up?"

"He's got an older brother, maybe a sister, too, but they don't live around here. Sylmar, maybe. He came to a game once, asked about his kid brother. I told him he was doing great. I'm not going to tell him that I worry that the kid is too quiet, too alone, that it's scary for a kid not to have a single friend on the team. It's not my place."

Rickie and the other players in the booth overhear all of this conversation; he sits with his head down looking intently at the empty glass in front of him. Finally, the boy sitting across from him says quietly, "That's not true, dude. We're your friends, aren't we?" The others nod or agree quietly. Rickie looks up at them gratefully, even though he knows it isn't true; he has done very little to encourage their friendship. Maybe he will try to do that during next season.

As he takes infield practice, Rickie notices Alex sitting in the stands. Alex is tall and muscular. He has a shaved head and a little goatee. His skin is dark and his eyes are black, and he looks sullen and menacing until he smiles. His smile is radiant, but Rickie suspects Alex rarely displays it because he fears it makes him look vulnerable.

Rickie gives Alex a quick nod as he heads out to second base to take infield practice.

Now Rickie knows what nags at him. It returns to the forefront of his mind as he picks up a slow roller and shovels it to the shortstop. He doesn't put enough on it and it falls at the shortstop's feet.

"C'mon, Rickie," Coach yells. "Get with it. Concentrate."

Oscar is bothering him.

Oscar from Pacoima, tall and light-skinned with a sharp, intolerant face, scoffs at the fact that Rickie and Alex stole a car; brags about gang-raping a young girl who'd been given something to knock her out at a party; says he robbed a 7-Eleven in San Fernando, and who served time in Juvy for almost kicking a kid to death.

"You alone?" Dennis had asked skeptically. Dennis is tall and thin like Oscar, but his face is uncomplicated and young. They were sitting on a bench at school in the shade; it's lunchtime.

"No, fool, a bunch of us."

"How many?" Tony asked. Tony and Dennis have never done anything except tag and shoplift. Tony is heavy and slow; he and

Dennis are best friends.

"I don't know. Five, six."

"Shit," Dennis said. "Anyone can do that. How'd you get caught?"

"The kid didn't die, and we didn't kick him hard enough in the head. He ID'd us."

The members of the crew don't talk about it openly, but everyone looks to Rickie. They know, too, that he has to do something to equal Oscar or in some subtle way, Oscar will take control. It aches in the pit of Rickie's stomach. The idea of joining five or six other people to rape a girl or kick a kid until he's almost dead holds no interest for him. That's bullying, what others wanted to do to him since he was a little boy. That's why he hates Oscar: he's like all of the kids he had to fight and beat up so that he wouldn't be beaten up instead. Mean and cowardly, depending on a group rather than fighting one on one, that's how people like Oscar fight. Rickie will have to beat him up, hurt him, hit him until someone pulls him off because that's the only way to ensure being left alone. Unless Oscar gets stupid and arms himself with a weapon. A kid did just that a couple of months before, brought a baseball bat to school, but the *vato* he attacked was twice his size. The bat only dazed him for a moment, and the assailant knew he was in trouble. He was grateful when the school cop caught him jumping the fence. He was put away in Juvy for a while.

Or like the dropout who came for someone after school and stood in the crosswalk brandishing a golf club. He even swung it at a female assistant principal. A driver who figured out what was going on and who was probably pissed at having to wait so long, drove right at the kid and knocked him down. The school cop subdued him, and the driver drove on.

If Oscar is dumb enough to come at him with a weapon, Rickie will have to beat him even worse. But even that won't be enough. He will have to do something that shows reckless disdain for human life and for the law, no matter whether Oscar's stories are true. And he will have to do it soon.

The team goes through practice listlessly, no matter how much Coach Vega yells at them.

Anger and frustration play across the coach's face as he stands in the batter's box leaning on the bat and watching the languid play of his team on the field.

"You guys look like you don't care out there."

When he gathers them around after practice, he says, "You got a big game tomorrow, and you don't look like you give a damn if you win or not. You think they're going to hand you the win? Think again. They're a good team. They're going to fight you to be in the championship. What is it? Too hot? Too tired? Is that it? Let's see how hot and tired you are. Five times around."

Everyone groans.

"If I see any slackers, it's another five for everyone. Let's go! On your feet. Now!"

They scramble to their feet and begin their jog around the field.

"Rickie," the coach calls. "Come over here."

Rickie walks toward the coach down the first baseline. The afternoon has begun to cool slightly now that the sun is low on the horizon. The scent of heated pine trees fills the air. Mockingbirds trill and whistle in the branches.

"You're supposed to be a leader out there. What's going on? Where's your spirit? Where's your hustle?" the coach asks.

"Laziness is unacceptable."

Rickie says nothing. He stands facing the coach looking down at his spikes.

"I need to count on you," Coach Vega says. When Rickie still doesn't respond, the coach says, "Well?"

"Okay, Coach, I'll do better."

"These guys need to see it from you, you understand?"

"Yeah. Sorry, Coach."

"Okay, do your laps. Let's go."

The sun has set by the time practice is over. Rickie approaches the bleachers where Alex is sitting slowly and without energy.

"You tired, fool?" Alex asks as they walk from the field.

"Yeah, I guess."

"You looked like your heart wasn't in it."

"It wasn't, dude. It's too hot. Coach was pissed. I don't blame him. I sucked today. I don't care."

Alex looks at him closely, startled by the bleakness of his friend's attitude. "Yeah, you do. Baseball's your life, your ticket out."

"That's a long shot," Rickie says dismissively. "Come on, let's go."

"Okay," Alex says as he stands. "If you say so. Hey, if baseball doesn't work out, we could both go to Mexico to my grandpa's *hacienda*. You could go with me, dude. It's beautiful there. We could work for him."

"You can't go there. You've got your mom and little sisters to take care of here. If you go, who takes care of them?" Rickie asks. Alex doesn't answer.

Alex is Rickie's only real friend. They have been friends since grade school. It doesn't bother Rickie that Alex feels responsible for him, but Alex is wary of him as well—Rickie does things impulsively, stupid things, like stealing the car when the guy had left it running to sprint into his house to answer the phone. A *veterano* no less. Rickie roped Alex into that one. They did their community service hours together cleaning up the school and formed a crew with Tony and Dennis.

"Not a gang. A crew. Crews are different," Rickie told his brother Bill. "Crews aren't gangs."

"What does your crew do?" Bill asked. "The same shit gangs do. Vandalize, tag, steal cars, who knows, maybe someday getting guns and shooting people. It's no good, *mi'jo*. You'll get yourself in big time trouble. You, too, Alex. What about your mother and sisters?"

"Where am I going to get guns?" Rickie asked, scoffing at his brother's worries.

"You should come work with me, Junior. Maybe both of you. They don't pay good, but at least it's a job. You could stay at my place," Bill offered.

"You have your parties, your girls. No way I want to be there listening to you snorting like a bull in the next room."

Rickie wanted Bill to insist, but he didn't. Instead, he looked at his younger brother and his friend and was silent. Rickie knew that Bill needed their grandfather, too, maybe more than any of them.

"Where's *abuelito* when you need him?" Bill asked out loud after Rickie was caught with the car. "I miss him and all his advice. Who's going to save us from ourselves?" Rickie looked at him curiously. What did he mean by that?

"You're probably right, Junior. I barely know what I'm doing, trying to figure shit out on my own; living my life is hard enough, much less yours or Alex's or Daisy's or *abuelita's*."

"You got a game tomorrow?" Alex asks.

"Yeah."

"What time?"

"Nine. I have to be there at eight-thirty."

"Who with?"

"The Red Sox. They've got that tall dude who can throw an eighty-mile fastball. They put the gun on him."

"*¡Hijole!* You ever hit him?"

"I struck out the first two times. I got a double the last time. Just put my bat out and the ball went into right field."

"What are you going to do now?"

"Go home and change."

"I know that, fool. After that."

"I don't know."

"You want to go meet up with Tony and them?" Rickie knows that Alex actually would prefer to stay home. It's safe there and he can relax and indulge in his dreams of going to Mexico.

"I guess so."

"Maybe we'll go to the UA and find some girls."

They walk through the neighborhood they have lived in since birth, past the elementary school they attended with its asphalt playground where they scraped knees and elbows and bloodied their mouths when they fell; with its low main building and added portable classrooms, all painted beige with blue doors; with its high fences and the sign out front which read "L st Day of S hool, Jun 21," because some of the letters have been stolen or blown away by the Santa Ana winds the previous week; past little block houses painted in faded colors with high wrought iron fences and wrought iron at the windows and heavy black security doors and dogs that charge the gate when people pass.

The boys turn down Rickie's street. It is cooler now. Friday. Young guys just home from work, or guys who don't have a job and have spent the day inside, are outside now, leaning against the long Chevys or Oldsmobiles or Buicks of twenty, thirty years ago. They gather in groups of three and four, beers in hand, in T-shirts, undershirts, or no shirts, with shaved heads and goatees and black sunglasses, brown torsos with tattoos in Old English across the shoulders or the lower back. They watch the boys pass silently; someone laughs after they have passed, but neither boy looks back. Older men water dry lawns, women sweep yards, music blares, and children run in the street.

"I'll meet you at Tony's house," Alex says when they reach the cross street midway down Rickie's street. Alex lives one block over.

"In about an hour."

"How come?"

"I'm tired, Homes. I need to take a shower, sleep a little."

"Okay, *pues*."

When Rickie arrives at the house, he hopes to find his brother's car parked out front. Rickie wants to get some food with his brother. Bill is the only person he feels strongly about other than his grandmother, and he feels mostly pity for her, pity mixed with anger at some anonymous "them" who make her life so hard and at himself for not being better for her. When Lopez asked the boys in the group if they could think of anyone they loved, Rickie thought of Bill with a tenderness that surprised him and brought tears to his eyes. He knew that Bill missed their grandfather, too, and he was having a hard time living on his own, without anyone to guide him.

When it was his turn to speak up, Rickie kept his head down and said he couldn't think of anyone.

But no car is parked in front, and the front door closes behind him with a sound that echoes through the empty house.

He tells himself he is only going to lie down for a minute, stretch his legs and relax his back, but soon he is in a deep sleep.

The weapon he's carrying he can't name but he knows it. He can picture it; he has used it in a video game. It is too heavy for him. His arms are being strained in their sockets. He is in a war zone, and the sky is the lurid orange of battle, of fire and smoke and sunsets. He has to find his squad leader to exchange this weapon for something lighter, but he can't find him in the ruined buildings which are just fragments of brick and mortar walls. It all looks like a scene out of an Xbox game, but there is real danger, not from bullets, but from something lurking behind one of the walls. So far, he has turned each corner without coming to harm. He has one more to turn, and he is terrified of what is waiting for him. He awakens as he is about to turn that corner. His T-shirt is soaked with sweat.

CHAPTER 6

All of the others are sitting in a line on the front steps when Rickie arrives at Tony's house. He opens the gate carefully, his eye out for the Rottweiler.

"He's in back," Tony says. "He wanted to chew Alex up." They all laugh except Alex.

"*Pinche perro*," Alex grumbles. "I hate that dog." He flicks dirt clods and stones with his thumb onto the brittle grass.

"So, what are we gonna do?" Dennis asks.

"What can we do?"

"Anyone got any money?"

"I got a little," Alex answers.

"I got some, too," Dennis says. "I got it out of my mom's purse."

"Asshole! Why'd you do that for? That might be food money," Tony says.

"Those people pay her good," Dennis says. He needs to defend himself. "She would've gave it to me anyway. She was asleep. What was I gonna do, wake her up? She'd a'been really pissed. I'll tell her later."

"How much we got?" Oscar asks. He stands and faces them. "Everybody give me theirs. I'll count it up." They hand him the money and he counts it slowly.

"Twenty-six bucks and twenty-nine cents."

"We could go to the UA. We gotta hurry. The cheap prices end pretty soon."

"I don't want to see no dumbass movies," Oscar says. The others look at him.

"What do you want to do?" Rickie asks. His stomach tightens. Tony and Dennis stand; Alex remains seated next to Rickie.

"I don't know. Something. You're like a bunch of little kids with nothing to do. Stealing money from your mommies. Going to the UA. What's that all about?" He stands away from the group, above them.

"Hey, fucker, what's *your* big idea?" Dennis asks angrily.

"You guys don't ever *do* anything. Why do we have a crew? I'm getting tired of just hanging out. I need some action."

"'I need some action.' You been watching too much TV, Homes."

"Yeah, well, what've *you* been doing besides jacking off?"

"Fuck you," Dennis says. He stares at Oscar.

"Relax, Dennis. It's too hot."

"Well, tell him to shut up."

Rickie stares at Oscar's face. He recognizes something there that scares him. Something dead. Something sightless and ugly. Oscar doesn't give a shit about anything. He's empty. That's what allowed him to kick a kid to unconsciousness and to gang rape a silly thirteen-year-old girl who thought that hanging out with tag bangers would be cool.

"I don't know why I asked to join this crew. You're a bunch of pussies. I'm going to…"

From his sitting position, Rickie lunges for him out of hate for the deadness he sees and the fear that it might have infected him, too. He's tired of Oscar's criticism, tired, too, of worrying that Oscar might be right about him, about his crew. He grabs Oscar's right calf with his left hand and jerks it up and slams hard with his open right hand on the other kneecap. Oscar loses his balance and goes down hard with a loud explosion of air. Immediately Rickie's on top of the taller boy and going for his face, wanting to tear out of him the condescension and the stone cold lack of feeling he sees there.

"Rickie!" Alex shouts and wraps his arms around him and pulls him off. Oscar gets up quickly and is about to run at Rickie, who's pinned in Alex's bear hug, but Dennis and Tony each grab and wrap up one of Oscar's arms.

They stand like this for a minute breathing heavily and watching one another. "Fuck, dude, what are you guys doing?" Alex asks, finally letting Rickie go when he feels him relax. "It's too hot!"

Oscar shakes himself out of Tony and Dennis's grasp. Neither Rickie nor Oscar speaks; they continue to eye one another warily, ready to respond if the other makes a move. Rickie and Alex sit down on the step; Oscar stands at a distance with Tony and Dennis at his sides. No one says anything.

"Dude, you're bleeding back here," Tony says, pointing to a spot on the back of Oscar's head. "I'll get you something." He goes inside the house and comes back out with a wet paper towel.

"It's cold. Put it on your face first. Your cheek is sort of messed up." Oscar touches his cheek, winces, and presses the wet towel there for a minute.

"Dude, what the fuck is with you?" he says to Rickie, but Rickie doesn't respond.

"Here, give it to me. I'll clean back here." No one says anything while Tony cleans the back of Oscar's head.

"So, what does anyone want to do?" Alex asks quietly when no one has spoken for a while.

"Nothin'. I just remembered: I gotta go to my little cousin's birthday party," Oscar says. He hands the money to Alex, removing the couple of dollars he put in, and brushes himself off.

"Well then? What's all the talk about doing something when you're going to some little kid's birthday party?" Dennis asks. "I don't get you, fool. You cause a bunch a crazy shit to happen and then tell everybody you got to go to a birthday party. That's fucked, dude. Who's the pussy now?"

After Oscar leaves, the other four sit and stand around for a few minutes and don't speak.

"That dude is crazy," Dennis says finally. "I don't trust him much. It's not *that* hot. Why'd he act like that?" He looks to Rickie, believing that he has the answer, but Rickie looks down at his hands and doesn't say anything. He shakes his head slightly. There's no way to explain it. It's something like a disease, something in the air or water or in the ground here, something larger than he is and more powerful and frightening. Something that makes you not care about anything, that makes you want to destroy things. What is it? He sees it in Oscar's eyes and knows that he'll always have to be on his guard around him.

"Patty's going to be at the UA," Alex finally says.

"How do you know?"

"She told me her mom was going to let her go."

"If Patty's there, maybe Claudia's mom will let her go, too. She trusts Patty. Marta and Michelle might come. I say we go. Maybe who knows," Dennis says. He has never had a real girlfriend even though he is tall and handsome. Girls, even the ones in his Special Ed. classes, see him as too childish, too much a little boy who still does goofy things to get attention.

The boys pool their money to get into the UA; they barely have enough for admission. They want popcorn and a soda but can't convince the kid they know from school to give them anything for the little they have left. He looks at them for a long time, but then catches the eye of the manager watching him and shakes his head.

All of the people who work there are classmates of the boys or just a year or two older. They wear a uniform of burgundy pants and pale yellow short-sleeved shirts that look as though they were bought for someone else, and they have plastic nametags on the breast pockets. They're from the neighborhood, except for the manager, and they know what it's like having nothing to do and having no money, no job, and no car. They turn a blind eye to most of what goes on—kids going from theater to theater, having sex in the back corners of the theaters, talking, putting their feet up on the seats. They think it's funny or just what kids do.

Alex finds an usher he knows, goes through an elaborate handshake, and asks if he has seen the girls yet. His friend shakes his head. The boys look for the girls in the lobby and check for them in the darkened theaters, but there's no sign of them.

"I bet Patty fought with her mom," Alex says. "They always fight. Patty can't keep her mouth shut."

They go from theater to theater. At some point Tony has half a bag of popcorn and a drink.

"Where'd you get that?"

"I found them on a seat." When the others laugh and tell him he's crazy, he says, "I checked them out. There's nothing in the popcorn. I'm hungry."

"How about the drink?" Dennis asks. "How about backwash?"

"Shit," Tony says and puts the drink down.

They leave after midnight, after watching parts of three movies. Their eyes burn. Rickie knows Coach Vega will be really pissed if he finds out that Rickie spent all night before a morning ballgame watching movies. He's always telling the team members to rest their eyes the night before a game so that they'll be sharp for hitting. If Rickie goes 0-for, Coach will know.

They don't see enough of the movies or don't care enough about them to talk about them afterwards. They stand in the lobby looking around for people they know, but there's no one.

"You want to do something?" Dennis asks.

"Yeah, eat. But we ain't got the money."

They push their way through the glass doors and stand on the sidewalk. The wind has begun to blow, tearing at the skinny trees planted in the squares of dirt cut out of the concrete. Papers, empty cups and plastic bags swirl around in the hot wind. A lone soda can rolls noisily against the curb and away again.

"We're going to have a fire," Alex says, looking toward the foothills for the telltale orange glow in the sky. Rickie looks as well, remembering his dream earlier.

"Fuck," Dennis says. "The wind just blew sand or some shit in my eyes." He stands with his head down, rubbing his eyes. The others turn their backs to the wind and begin to walk backwards.

"I'm going home," Rickie says. "I've got that playoff game tomorrow."

"Yeah, I'm going, too," Alex says. "I don't want to stay here."

The four of them walk with their heads down, away from the shops and stores and well-lighted streets into the neighborhood.

It's a dangerous time—after midnight, walking home on poorly lit streets. Easy targets for drive-bys. They walk warily, watching each car as it passes, turning to look at any car approaching from the rear. Each boy picks up a rock to carry concealed in the hand away from the street. Most cars drive by silently, faces staring at this group of four boys. Some people yell at them, call them names and laugh.

Finally, one car slows and the rider in the front passenger seat leans out the open window. Here it comes, Rickie thinks. The shots—they sound almost insignificant, almost harmless. Not loud retorts, but a sort of sputter, a popping. Then flesh will tear, the searing pain, the surprising blood.

The boys freeze, unable to do anything other than be spectators or victims of whatever is going to happen next.

"What are you little boys doing out so late? It's past your bedtime, ain't it? Where're you from?"

No one answers. They begin to walk again, heads down.

"I said, where're you from? Too scared to answer? Too sleepy?" The voice waits. "I got something to wake you up." The lowered Chevy painted in grey primer lurches ahead and stops, goes at a crawl again. "You'll love this," the voice calls. He throws something out the window. Simultaneously, someone else in the car says loudly, "Oh, shit," and the car speeds away.

Whatever they throw hits the sidewalk. The boys run. Tony,

overweight and clumsy, trips and hits the ground hard. A deafening explosion. Rickie waits for the pain as he runs down the sidewalk. Nothing. Cherry bomb or an M-80. A police car races by, its siren just beginning to whoop. Another pulls up.

"Over here. Quick. You. Get back here. Hands up. On the hood. Quick. Get up, kid. Right now."

The boys do as they're told. Tony rubs his forehead, his face contorted; he looks like he wants to cry. A blow to each ankle kicks their legs apart. Outside lights and living room lights go on. People come out to stand at their doors, wakened by the explosion, the sirens, the yelling. The boys lean over the hood of the police car in the glow of the flashing blue and red lights.

"Are we going to find anything illegal in your pockets?"

The boys shake their heads. The cops pat them down, remove their wallets from their pockets.

"I.D.'s?" the older cop asks. The younger one hands the ID's to the older. He gets back inside the car.

"Where you coming from?"

"The UA," Tony says in an injured voice. "Just walking home. Not doing nothing."

The cop who asks the question is young, maybe not even thirty yet. He has a scar on the right side of an otherwise smooth, handsome face that goes from the corner of his mouth up his cheek almost to his eye. The scar pulls his mouth slightly into a permanent look of puzzlement. He looks at the boys mildly, without the stony contempt they often encounter from school police or other North Hollywood Division officers.

"How many shows did you guys see?" he asks to relieve the tension.

"Three," Alex offers.

"Mmm," he says. "Used to do that, too." Rickie reads the name on his badge—Padilla. "Couldn't do it now. Hurts my eyes."

No one responds, unused as they are to this kind of conversation from a cop. He, in turn, is made uncomfortable by their silence and looks at his partner in the car.

"We were just walking home," Alex says, realizing that they might have missed an opportunity. "No one's got a license, no car. You know. We weren't doing anything, sir. Those guys..."

"I know. We've been chasing them around for a while now. I don't think they have anything except for the cherry bombs. No weapons." His partner gives him a thumbs-up sign from inside the patrol car.

"You guys can relax now."

Thinking that they can relax because the people in the car don't have weapons, the boys still don't move their hands from the hood of the car.

"No, I mean, you can take your hands down and turn around. You can sit down over there," he says gesturing to the yard of the house they're in front of.

They do as they're told.

"Hey," the cop says to Rickie, "I seen you before."

Thinking the cop recognizes him from when he was arrested for joyriding up in the canyon, Rickie tenses. They're going to check on him even more. He'll get the lecture at least. He says nothing. He looks down at his shoes. They'll get Alex in a moment.

"You play ball, don't you? Yeah, I thought I seen you," he says when Rickie nods. "Over here at the park? My little brother plays on the Red Sox. Yeah."

No one speaks. Rickie doesn't offer that he's playing the cop's brother's team the next day. Padilla realizes he has been too friendly and backs up a few steps from the boys. His partner gets out of the car. "Mr. Trujillo and Mr. Hernandez," the older cop calls. The boys look up. "Are you staying out of other people's cars?" Rickie nods. The cop stares at him silently for a minute. "Yes, sir," Alex says. "We are."

"Okay. You guys head on home."

"Where do you live?" Padilla asks as he hands the boys their wallets.

"Over on Benton," Dennis offers.

"Not too far," the young cop says.

"Remember. You guys are violating curfew. We're going to let you go on that, but double time it home. If we come back and find you still hanging around, we're going to ticket you, got it?" the older cop, Sanchez, says.

The boys nod.

Sanchez struts slowly back to the driver's side pushing down on his belt as he walks. The Kevlar vest inside his shirt makes everything tight and uncomfortable.

"Straight home, guys. Remember," Padilla says.

When both cops are back in the car with the door closed, Rickie says, "Fuck you." The others look at him curiously.

"*Calmate*, Homes. Shut up. Don't be an asshole," Alex says.

Rickie makes a noise of disgust. "You're the asshole, man. All cops are the same, the ones who beat on you and the ones who act nice. And we're all the same to them. Garbage. Don't let them fool you."

"Did you see the scar on that dude's face?" Dennis asks. "My uncle's got one just like it. His old man, my grandpa, took a broken bottle to him when he was drunk. *Abuelito* cries every time he sees that scar."

"That shit was ugly," Tony says.

"He knew you, Rickie," Dennis says, impressed with Rickie's celebrity.

"So? What's your point?"

"No point, dude. Just he knew you from playing baseball. I thought that was cool. Calm down, Rickie."

When he gets home, Rickie goes into the living room. He knows he will find *abuelita* asleep on the couch with the TV still on. He watches for a minute—some guy singing in Spanish, the girls in back of him with their breasts almost pushed out of the tops of their dresses. He checks to see what he thinks about them. Too tired.

He covers his grandmother with the crocheted blanket on the back of the sofa and switches off the TV. He walks in darkness to his room. Blue-white light from the street edges past the shade and glints off the trophies on the dresser and their mirror images. He is too agitated to turn on a light or take off his clothes. He kicks his shoes off and lies back on the bed and stares at the ceiling with his hands behind his head. Angry. Angry at being tricked into running away from a cherry bomb. Angry at being stopped, at being recognized. What did that cop think he was doing by buddying up to Rickie? He doesn't give a shit that his kid brother plays on the Red Sox. Angry, too, at the ugliness of the scar. It revolted him, made him almost physically sick looking at it. And the cop was calm about it, like it didn't make a difference. He should hide his ugly face away from people, and work in an office behind a closed door.

When these thoughts subside, Rickie becomes conscious of a conversation going on in his head, a heated one, almost an argument, but he can't identify the speakers or what they're saying. He knows he is the subject and that he really should listen because it's important, but rather than get closer and clearer to him, the conversation moves off into the distance and is lost in the enfolding darkness.

CHAPTER 7

This morning Berta remembers. She goes through the events of the past as though they are beads on the Rosary she holds in her hands. She recalls each event carefully before passing on to the next. She sits at the kitchen table with the back door open, welcoming in the cooler morning air. Nothing is before her but a cup of strong black coffee. She has time before she catches the bus. Today she works in Burbank.

"Don't arrive before ten, Berta. Saturday's my day to sleep in," Mrs. Whitcolm told her. "You sleep in, too," she added, but Berta rises at her usual early hour and sits at the kitchen table with her coffee. She wears a shapeless dark blue dress and blue cardigan sweater. The women whose houses she cleans give her clothes, some of which she wears, most of which she gives away at church because they do not fit or are not appropriate for her. She and other women from the neighborhood find their clothes on the hangers in the church storage room or in the bags by the wall outside.

The parishioners line up on Friday afternoons. When the gate is opened precisely at two o'clock, they rush to tear open the black garbage bags to see what clothing they contain. Occasionally Berta is lucky to discover a good dress in her size. She does not care if the dresses are a little worn, as long as they are proper. The women of today seem to have no sense of that. She thinks of the women who have carried many children, but who still wear tight shorts and T-shirts, the rolls of stomach showing in the gap between the shirt and shorts. She sees them pushing their mountains of laundry to the *lavanderia* in shopping carts, a string of little girls in tow, holding hands as they cross the street.

Don't they know how they look? And the girls of today, what they don't show!

She doesn't understand.

Home, her real home, is half a continent away. Her husband is dead. Her son, Ricardo, lives somewhere in Ventura or Santa Barbara, she doesn't know.

Ricardo was seven years old when she and her husband, Osvaldo, made it to this country. They gave up everything, almost gave up their lives on the journey from Sinaloa to Tijuana, from Tijuana to San Diego and finally to Los Angeles.

He was so vibrant, Osvaldo, so full of hope and determination. He never looked back, never longed for home as she did. Or, if he did, he never spoke to her about it. "Our life is here," he would say. He was so different from everyone else, from all of those who made no secret of their disappointment with the United States. He learned everything—brick-laying and stone-work, tile-laying, carpentry, plumbing, roofing, and so much more. He free-lanced as a handyman, stood on street corners with others and sometimes, particularly in the early days when he didn't know any better, took almost nothing for his work. He knew he could never say he didn't know how to do something, so with a sharp eye he watched and learned fast, and when the white men pulled up to the corner in their pick-up trucks and asked him something in English, he nodded and said, "*Sí, yo puedo.*"

He stood near a truck rental yard and spent hours waiting in the soaking rain or in the strong sun, breathing air that choked him, flagging down every truck that came or went, seeking narrow shelter in the shadow of a lamp post or the eave of a convenience store; too many of those days brought little or no work.

They lived in a garage then, the three of them. On the days when he had not worked, he returned home after dark, downcast but not defeated. Berta had *frijoles* and tortillas warm and ready for him, and she listened to the story of his day, about who got work and who besides him did not. The food revived him and he found some reason to speak hopefully of the next day. "Tomorrow is Monday. It is a day that many people begin jobs. There will be work." Or, "Tomorrow is Saturday. There will be work for everyone tomorrow." And often he was lucky, luckier than many. Perhaps it was because she washed and ironed his shirts and creased his pants every day. Perhaps it was because, other than his pencil-line mustache, he was clean-shaven every day. Or perhaps it was his indomitable good nature and unshakable belief that everything would be all right soon, so apparent on his face and in his every gesture, that caused men to stop and motion for him to come over to the truck first of all. Then they told him how many others as well.

And he returned home on those evenings with a pocketful of money. They put some aside for the landlord in an old purse of

Berta's, which she hid under her clothes in a cardboard box. Then they went to the store and bought carefully, mostly dry goods— beans and rice and flour and coffee. Some lard. A little milk, a few fresh vegetables, some oranges for Ricardo. A *paleta* for each of them. *Pan dulce* for the morning coffee.

They all slept together on a double bed mattress in the winter, glad to be close for the warmth in that uninsulated garage. During the summer and early autumn, the heat was intense in there. They had no windows to open, only the door, but Berta was afraid to leave it open at night for fear of robbers who would steal the money she safeguarded in her brown purse.

Osvaldo rose before light and dressed quietly. She made coffee for him and tortillas and heated more of the *frijoles* by the dim light of a lamp the landlord had given them. He had given them the mattress, as well, both of which he factored into the rent. He was from Jalisco, but he had been in America for twenty years; a large man with a smile he turned on and off at will, and a cold disdain for recent arrivals because he was convinced they would upset the delicate equilibrium of his relationship to the white Americans. "They don't have money. They come here to get the Welfare. Their kids grow up like wild animals, join gangs, have babies at fourteen." He dismissed the other Mexican immigrants as worthless, but saved his complete disdain for the immigrants from the other Central American countries. They were scum who came here only to become criminals.

"You look at your gang members," the landlord would say to anyone who would listen. "They are from El Salvador, Honduras and Guatemala. They bring only trouble here." And his white listeners, who couldn't differentiate one immigrant from the next, had their beliefs confirmed that only a handful of immigrants were good enough to do menial jobs and the rest were a drain on the economy.

After Osvaldo left in the mornings, Berta sat in the dim light with her coffee and waited for the time to pass until she woke her son. She made sure to dress him in clean clothes and feed him in the morning. When he had washed his face and hands and brushed his teeth, and she had combed his hair, she walked him the five blocks to school. She left him with the exhortation to "Do good" and the promise that she would be there to meet him after school. And she always was, even during the days of torrential rains and flooded streets.

She stood across from the school beneath a big black umbrella she struggled with in the wind, her shoes and knee-high stockings and hem of her long skirt soaked from crossing the streets, and waited until Ricardo came running. The two of them trudged home on the wet sidewalks, laughing and dodging the deepest puddles, and dried their clothes as best they could with the little space heater, which took so much electricity that it caused the landlord to shake his head and threaten to raise the rent when he saw the electric bill.

Berta and Ricardo followed the same routine each day through elementary school, and though she worried that he was learning too much English because she feared it would separate him from his father and her, yet Ricardo was her shining star, her hope, and her devotion. He would fit in here in America. He would understand things and explain them to her and to Osvaldo. Ricardo would stand between them and the complex, fast-moving life around them, and he would protect them from it.

After the first weeks of walking with her to middle school, Ricardo told her not to do it any more because it embarrassed him. He had made new friends and they would walk together. So she stood at the curb in the mornings and watched him join his friends at the corner. At first he looked back and waved but that stopped soon as well.

Osvaldo got a job driving a forklift at a forge in South Gate and doing maintenance for the grounds and the offices, whatever job needed to be done. A year later, they were able to move out of the garage, though not before paying the landlord extra money. He was angry that they had found the means to move out from under his control, and he issued veiled threats that he might have "to speak to the authorities" about them, or that he might have to look into Osvaldo's new job, talk to his boss. About what? they asked. But the landlord only shrugged. So they paid for unspecified damage or for having given short notice or for something, and lived in fear in their new little apartment that someone would come knocking and send them back to Mexico.

No one came. The job continued. Ricardo finished middle school and went on to high school. Berta's hopes diminished with Ricardo's poor grades and his growing interest in girls. She hoped that he would read to them in Spanish, maybe teach them a little more English, but he was scornful of that, moody and bad-tempered, and she left him alone.

Then they were able to buy this small house, and she had little time to think about Ricardo. He was in high school and, *Dios mío*, was out of her control. He didn't listen any more, hardly spent any time at home after his friends got cars. What was she to do? This little house took so much time!

Ricardo finished high school and got a job right after graduation at a food warehouse where all his friends worked. Soon he announced that his girlfriend, Esmeralda, was pregnant. Ricardo wanted the girl to just move in, but Berta insisted on a marriage. A wedding was arranged. Her family paid for most of it, but the newlyweds would live with Osvaldo and Berta until after the baby.

At the reception at the bride's parents' house, she and Osvaldo ate and drank and danced like all the others throughout the warm summer evening. They watched the young people dance with little grace to the American music that seemed to have no melody, just a primitive drum beat, and to the other American music where it sounded like angry people yelling and accusing and threatening. She and Osvaldo only danced to the beautiful Mexican love songs. Most of the time they watched everyone drink their Corona or Budweiser beer and listened to them speak English, not a beautiful language as they spoke it, but dull, without song, full of profane short words like explosions. These beautiful people, children and adults, elegant in their dresses and rented tuxedos, the women with their long hair pulled back to give full view to fine-boned Spanish faces or dark Indian faces, the bloodlines running back to Mayan or Aztec ancestors so clear in the round faces, wide mouths, full lips, small noses, and black eyes... These beautiful people sounded so different when they uttered this language. It didn't fit their faces, disfiguring them in some subtle way, she thought.

After the wedding Esmeralda moved in. Berta knew with a kind of dread what would happen, and it did. At first Ricardo was solicitous of the girl's health and comfort, and they stayed by themselves in their room with the door shut. He was constantly draped over her back or she hung on him. But as she grew bigger and more demanding, they spent more time in the living room watching the television sullenly, barely speaking to one another.

He worked more and more overtime. She spent most of her days watching the *novelas* and talking on the phone with girlfriends:

—What are you doing right now?

—Nothin', just talking with you.

—What's up with Marcela? How come she never calls or comes over your house?

—Her? She's all hot now with her new boyfriend and his truck.

—I hated her in tenth grade. She thought she was so all that.

—What're you gonna do tonight?

—Nothin'. Watch TV. It's nothin' but boring here.

—Me, too.

—Maybe we could go to the mall this weekend.

They spent their time talking secretively on the phone and with a lot of school-girl giggling, while Ricardo worked longer hours and spent more time with his friends away from the house. Esmeralda gained more weight. Ricardo sometimes came home smelling of beer or marijuana, but he always claimed other people were drinking beer and smoking; he never touched marijuana, he said.

Then the baby came. They named him Bill and called him Billy; Billy, not Osvaldo as Berta had hoped. Bill. Who was Bill, she wondered? What sort of name was that? Ricardo was home more for a while. Berta taught the girl how to care for the baby, but she often carried him slung sideways across her hip. Esmeralda took the baby to the mall with her girlfriends, and they sat together on benches and smoked and ate chips and drank soda and kept half an eye on their babies. Berta encouraged the girl to go for walks on the nice days or sit outside in the sun, but Esmeralda seldom did.

More and more Berta took care of the baby because the girl ignored him. Berta told the little one with the large eyes about the *pueblo* that was home for *abuelito* and her, and about the *hacienda*. She sang songs to him that she made up about the horses which ran in the corral from the sheer joy of being alive; of the snug little house; of the trees that the breeze played in as it lulled little babies to sleep; and of the sky filled with a million stars at night like diamonds scattered on black velvet. And the baby listened quietly in her arms and watched her with black understanding eyes.

Before she lost any of the weight from the first pregnancy, Esmeralda was pregnant again, and she wore it as a badge of honor to be pregnant with her second. She spent more time with her friends at their houses or in the living room of Berta's house, but mostly at the mall, dragging Billy around with her. She was tired frequently, and she hit the baby hard if he cried, or she yanked him by his arm if he was tired or hungry. Berta spoke to her, and the girl told her that the little boy was being bad.

Daisy was the second one. Berta didn't question the names. One day, soon after the second baby was born, Ricardo spoke to her.

—Don't have hurt feelings, 'Amá. We thought about naming her after you, but Berta is a name the Americans don't use any more. That's what the nurse said. She laughed when Esmy told her we were thinking about that name. Esmy asked her,—What about Flor?—How about Daisy? the nurse said, and we liked it. It's not 'cause we didn't want to name her after you. You understand, 'Amá, don't you?

After a while, everything went back to what it had been, except that the house felt more crowded. Osvaldo loved the babies.

Berta loved the babies. Their parents were babies themselves, the two older people agreed; it was just as well that they, Berta and Osvaldo, raised the children.

A few years passed. Ricardo and the girl hardly spoke to one another or spent any time together, but they didn't fight. They were like boarders, strangers to one another, except that they went into the same room to sleep. They never spoke of moving out.

One morning three years later, Esmeralda came out of the bathroom and went into the bedroom she and Ricardo shared. She yelled at him and they argued behind the closed bedroom door. When he came out, he announced to Berta that Esmeralda was pregnant again.

They named this baby Ricardo Jr. and called him Junior. They moved into the garage, which Osvaldo and Ricardo converted into a beautiful bedroom, not like the draughty garage he and Berta and Ricardo had lived in years before.

When Bill was thirteen, Daisy was twelve and Junior was nine, Ricardo left.

He left a letter for all of them in which he said that he could not stand living there any more. He was going to go up to Ventura to find a better job, maybe go back to school. He would send them an address and send money for the kids. After a few months of silence, postal money orders started arriving. They were never for much, but it was something.

Even after three or four months, he had not sent an address or called. Berta and Osvaldo could not understand until a young man came by the house asking for him. They told him that they didn't have an address or phone number.

—No wonder, the man said.—Did he tell you he had my sister?

—No, they said.

—She's fourteen.

—He took her? He stole her? They were horrified.

—No, not really. She wanted to go with him. She thought she loved him. What does a fourteen-year-old girl know?

—Where is she now?

—Back home.

—Is she..? Berta could not bring herself to ask.

—No, thank God.

What did he want with a girl that age?

Berta felt hope drain away. They had come far, far from home. She longed for the simplicity of the little house she had grown up in, with its clean-swept dirt floors and low ceiling and the pungent smell of mesquite wood burning in the stove and the sour smell, almost human, of tortillas and *frijoles* in the morning; the low door one passed through into the world outside, chickens pecking in the yard and horses coming up to the fence of the corral nickering for food, the dog lying in the weak sunshine of a winter morning and the mist rising off the land to reveal fields and a guava tree and a pomegranate and mountains blue in the distance. Days of hard, sure work were followed by evenings spent promenading in the plaza to cool down and chat with the others of the *pueblo*. Children ran about, dogs barked, young men spoke quietly to young women and the young women passed on without speaking but with smiles on their lips or expressions of disdain.

Couples disappeared in the crepuscular light. Often there were hurried weddings, and sometimes there were betrayals and wailing and fights under the trees, even shootings and funerals for passionate young men or unfortunate young women or children taken by God. But *She* was there always to look after them, their sweet, quiet *Virgencita*, their Dark Madonna. She did not look to the heavens or to a child. She looked down upon *all* her children with infinite compassion in her eyes and in her hands joined in supplication. She had issued from their land, from *la raza*—skin of their skin, bone of their bone, of their heart and their soul. She and she alone understood them and gave order and reason to existence. If they sustained loss, endured great sadness or enjoyed great happiness and birth, it was all in a world under her watchful eye.

But here, in the United States, life was too busy, too noisy, too fast. It was too *much*. There was no center, just a swirling storm of things and noise and obligations and papers spinning around nothing. Her son had been torn away from her, and she had no resources with which to call him back. Her *Virgén* was so small here, so distant, without power. And the other one, the one here in this country with her white skin, She looked to Heaven or at the Son in her arms. This Virgin didn't know, though maybe she tried; Berta thought maybe She didn't care about her brown-skinned children. No, God forgive her, She must. Maybe She, too, got lost or confused in the fast pace and the noise.

Esmeralda and the children stayed on with Berta and Osvaldo. Esmeralda was hysterical for weeks, crying night after night like some wounded animal. Berta tried to comfort her, but soon she realized that the girl did not want to get over Ricardo's leaving. At first, she spoke to her friends often on the phone, crying and cursing him, but soon the friends didn't call and when she called them, they seemed to have something pressing to do. Her parents moved away to a condominium in Santa Clarita. The children could visit, of course, and play on the swings and seesaws in the small play area in front of the complex, but there was not enough room for them to actually stay there. They sent Esmeralda money regularly.

And then one day about three months later, Esmeralda herself disappeared. She had been going out a couple of evenings a week, alone, but Berta was sure she was meeting someone. Berta expected something to happen, but not that the girl would leave entirely, deserting the children with no word. When they asked, Berta lied and told them that their mother had gone to Mexico to visit her grandparents for a while. She would be back.

"He doesn't want Ricardo's children," Esmeralda explained to Berta when she finally did return. She explained that she had found a new man. "You understand. I need to start life over again, too. I want to have his babies. I won't ever stop loving these kids," she said when tears started in Berta's eyes. "I'll always be there for them. I'll give you money. I'll come see them every week."

For a while, Esmeralda was good to her word. She came one afternoon each week and spent time until dinnertime in the house. Bill and Daisy often had homework to do and didn't spend much time with her. Junior sat with her, answered her questions in monosyllables, but he, too, had homework. She offered to help him. They sat on the sofa and spread his books and papers out on the coffee table. Sometimes he sat back in moody silence, and she grew irritated with him. She felt sorry for herself.

"I came here to see you, and this is how you are? What a way is that to treat your mom?" she asked, but he didn't respond. If he could have found the words, he would have told her that she didn't have a big place in his heart; she was a visitor. As long as he had his *abuelita* and *abuelito*…

Esmeralda did as well by them as she could, Berta thought,

but she was still a girl who didn't really know anything. Berta knew she would stop coming around if her children ignored her, and she did. Berta didn't blame her and neither did Osvaldo. He was glad to have children in the house to sit with him in the evenings at the kitchen table when he got home from work and had his dinner. He listened to their stories about school with wonderment and real interest, eager to hear about their friends and what they were learning, ready to laugh when they told him about yelling teachers or fights, ready to have his faith in them confirmed by attendance awards or good grades, ready to pass out dollar bills to hard workers. And until each of them reached middle school, Berta walked them to school in the rain and the heat.

Two years after Esmeralda left, Osvaldo began experiencing the pain "down there," and numerous trips to the clinic followed, and hours of sitting in waiting rooms and tests and weeks of waiting, and then the horrible pronouncement of cancer. In spite of the pills that made him sick and the vomiting and the blood, he went to work and hid the pain for as long as he could, and he refused to admit the fact that he was growing weaker by the day. But the day came when he had to quit and stay home.

He grew thinner, able to sit only for short periods of time and then on cushions. He spent more and more time lying on the sofa or in bed. He worried what would happen to them, but Berta told him to rest, she would find work. Hadn't she always kept a nice house? Couldn't she speak to her friends who cleaned houses for the white women? She did, and because she was pleasant and a hard worker, she found plenty of work. He could take his pills and rest.

In the evenings Berta returned late. She always feared the worst, but often she found him lying awake in their bed surrounded by the children. Daisy made dinner for them all. Bill sat with him and read to him from *La Opinión*. Junior sat silently on the edge of the bed and stared at him as though to will him back to good health, and then to prepare himself for what was sure to come. He didn't touch him unless his grandfather took his hand in his own. "It's okay, *mi'jo*," his grandfather said to him often. "I'll be back at work in no time."

Even at the end, Osvaldo talked about getting up and going to work, his poor face so drawn, his body so wasted away. Berta caressed his forehead and told him to rest; he had worked hard all his lifetime, and it was time to relax.

She returned one day to find the police and the coroner at the house, and she knew. She took the little money she had been saving for this occasion and buried him at the Mission cemetery. Neighbors helped. It was almost like being home again, the way they offered help without being asked, the way they came around with a few dollars here and there, food, and a sympathetic word. The women she cleaned for were saddened and some gave her extra money. Of course there was no way to get in touch with Ricardo.

That was four years ago. Nowadays, Bill is on his own and working, Daisy is on her own and going to college, and Junior is in high school. Berta has saved a little money during those four years. In a couple of years Junior will be through with high school. She can sell the house and move back to Mexico. She will take Osvaldo's body with her and bury him at home. She will live with her sister. She will be considered rich there. Her journey away from home will be over. She will be back in the land she knows, whose pace and tempo, whose colors and smells are still in her blood. She will be back in the embrace and care of her sweet dark Madonna.

CHAPTER 8

Rickie arrives at the field in time for the warm-up. His teammates greet him, but no one comes over to him. They call from where they stand in the field or near the batter's box.

"Hey, fool."

"You ready, Rickie?"

"I told you he'd be here on time, Coach."

"What's goin' on, Rickie?"

"Take second, Rickie, and warm up," the coach calls to him from home plate. Rickie keeps his head down as he runs out onto the field, not wanting the coach to see the dark circles under his eyes.

"All right, you guys, let's take some infield. Bobby, take the outfielders and hit some flies. Jose, you and Angel and Frankie go to the batting cage. No screwing around," he yells at their backs as they run to the cage to be first. "Practice stroking the ball. Swing level."

"Yeah, Angel, practice your stroke, fool," someone from bench calls, and the boys next to him laugh.

Rickie watches the three of them run for the batting cage, elbowing each other out of the way, like kids.

The infielders wait for Coach Vega. He hits an easy ground ball to Rickie, who handles it cleanly and throws on to first. One for the shortstop. Third. First. One for the catcher. Third. The ball doesn't come up for the third baseman but runs under his glove into left.

"Did you eat too much of your *mamá's* good cooking last night, Beto?" Coach calls to him. "You gotta get down for those. Okay, turn the double play."

He hits to Rickie, harder this time, just to the right field side of second base. He gets there quickly, takes the ball on a low bounce and shovels it to the shortstop covering. Coach Vega looks over at the coach of the opposing team. When they make eye contact, Rickie's coach shrugs and the other coach shakes his head in wonderment.

There are no dugouts at the field. The team members sit on benches behind the fence. In back of them, on both sides of the field, there are bleachers for the fans. Since this is a semi-final game, the bleachers on both sides fill early. Rickie's team, the Braves, sits on the first base side. The opposing team, the Red Sox, sits on the third base side, and the players have to look into the morning sun. The few Red Sox players who are finished with their warm-up sit on the bench with the bills of their caps pulled low. Spectators shade their eyes with a hand or, if they're lucky, a piece of cardboard they find near the snack bar.

By the third inning, the Braves are ahead by a run. Rickie gets on by an error his first time up, ducking a high hard fastball. The ball hits his bat and rolls out to the shortstop, who charges and throws in the dirt to first, the ball skipping by the first baseman and rolling all the way to the fence. The runner in front of Rickie, who walked, comes all the way home.

The game moves into the later innings. The boy with the fastball loses the plate and walks in two runs. The Red Sox change pitchers. At his next turn at the plate, Rickie hits a fly ball deep to right. The right fielder goes back, turns the wrong way, turns back and catches the ball. He holds the glove and ball aloft in triumph. Rickie trots back to the bench.

"Hey, *ese*, good hit. That dude's *lucky*, dude!" says a heavy-set young man seated in the stands behind the team. He wears dark sunglasses that cause red indentations along his temples to his ears on his shaved head. He is dressed in a white over-sized T-shirt and creased khakis. He often attends an inning or two of a game before wandering off. He is usually drunk.

"C'mon, de la Torre, tell us a story," he yells at the next batter. "If you're brown, you're down, *ese*," he calls to no one. "Where the hell are Sandra and Rosie?" he asks the two other young men with him. They, too, have shaved heads and wear large, white T-shirts and black sunglasses. They don't respond. Instead, they stand and head for the other side.

"Hey, where're you *mensos* going? Sandra and Rosie are going to be here. Was it something I said?" he asks and laughs.

"We're going to find Hector," one of them calls back.

"Hector the Collector," he says.

The Braves head for the field.

"What's the pitcher's name?" he calls to the three players sitting on the bench. Rickie hesitates before he takes the field. "Hey, what's the pitcher's name?"

"Gabe," Rickie calls up to him.

"Abe? C'mon, Abe, honest Abe, get the save."

"Gabe," Rickie calls.

"Gabe?"

"Gabe. *Gabriel*," he says, pronouncing it as a Spanish name.

"Oh, Gabe. My bad. C'mon, Gabe, get the save," he yells. "I'm an asshole mother-fucker," he says more to himself, but loudly enough to be heard. "Where're Sandra and Rosie? What the fuck?" he says as though speaking to someone seated near him, though no one is.

"Hey, man, I've got little kids here!" a father yells from a few rows above. The father stares warily at the back of his head, but the young man doesn't turn around. He sits hunched over and drops spit on the board at his feet. In a moment he gets up without looking back or saying anything and heads for the other side. People seated around the man who spoke up give him nods of approval. Everyone relaxes.

Rickie takes the field and surveys the stands as he waits for the first Red Sox hitter of the inning. He looked the players over earlier and tried to find the cop's brother. He thinks it might be the shortstop, the kid coming to bat now. He looks serious and intent on the game, as though there isn't much in life that is fun or funny. Rickie knows that he looks the same way to other people. Often adults whom he doesn't know, hasn't ever seen before, fans or parents of other players, tell him to lighten up and enjoy himself. He just looks at them when they say that.

He scans the crowd in search of the cop but doesn't find him, at the same time relieved and disappointed that he is not there. The cop has to be working. He isn't the kind of guy to miss his little brother's game if he doesn't have to. Rickie feels a surge of regret and self-pity, but he will not name the cause. Instead, he looks at the faces in the crowd again. There are a lot of fans his age and younger, brothers and sisters of the players or friends from school. Nice kids, quiet, not trouble-makers or kids who are very well known; kids who have gotten through middle school without calling attention to themselves, who will get through high school in the same way and then go on to junior college. Rickie envies them their invisibility, even resents their ability to get through without ever being noticed or remembered. Where will they end up? In jobs at hospitals or nursing homes; as teachers' aides, as secretaries or paralegals. They will come and go and no one will know them very well, just like Rickie's brother Bill and his sister Daisy. Rickie feels the fear of anonymity shiver through him. He wants to be elusive but not unknown, like James Bond, smooth, known for his artfulness in subduing villains and manufacturing escapes, universally admired by beautiful women and men alike.

So far, it is all just a stupid daydream. People know him, all right, but it's because trouble seems to find him. Like the time with the car. Or with Maltrey. He hadn't wanted those things to happen. They just did. He doesn't even remember very well what exactly happened, even minutes later. What did he say to Maltrey? Why? What did the teacher actually say? And he had to ask Alex exactly what happened when they took the car. When Alex told him, Rickie listened in a sort of dumbfounded admiration.

"I did that, fool?" he asks. "I did that? What was I thinking?"

"I don't know, you idiot," Alex says with a wry laugh, "but we gotta stay off that street. That fool will kill us if he ever sees us again."

Rickie shakes himself out of his reverie. He looks at the other people in the stands. Parents and relatives of the players and old men come to watch the kids play in the cooler morning. And on the top row now, Rickie's sister Daisy sits all by herself.

What is she doing here? When did she get here? She didn't tell him she was coming. He is angry about that but quietly glad that she has come to see him play. He looks for Bill. No sign of him. Daisy sees that he notices her, sees also the glance in search of someone else. She waves bravely to Rickie, who nods almost imperceptibly to her and turns his attention to the batter.

Rickie handles everything hit his way easily and effortlessly. In his last at-bat, he hits a double in the gap between right and center, driving in another run and scoring himself when the next batter singles. The kid coaching third tries to hold him up, but Rickie knows that most players don't have accurate arms and that most catchers can't move very well. The ball is thrown to the first base side of home and the catcher doesn't get back in time to tag him out. He scores standing up.

"Rickie. Pay attention to the third base coach, *amigo*," Coach Vega says when Rickie comes back to the bench. The boy nods without speaking.

"Let's talk soon," Coach says to him. "After the season. I want to talk with you about your future, okay? About college. You can do it, *mi'jo,* but you have to give it your all. You have to start now. Concentrate on getting good grades. Work on your skills."

"Okay, Coach," Rickie says. He wants to please the man, but how can he do it when he has already lost so much enthusiasm for the game? Coach can see it in the slump of his shoulders and his expressionless face.

"Let's talk seriously about the future before…" He wants to add, "before it's too late," but the talk ends when the weakest batter on the team gets a base hit.

The Braves win the game easily. The players are jubilant, shouting and high-fiving. Even Rickie high-fives a player, the shortstop, Manuel.

"Okay. Everyone gather around," the coach calls. They all stand around the first baseline. "Tomorrow is Sunday. No practice, no game, but I thought I might come out mid-morning and hit some flies, give you a little infield, pitch some batting practice. Nothing serious. Just easy. What do you say?" He is speaking to the whole team, but he is looking at Rickie. "I'll even take you for donuts afterwards. On me. Is it a yes?"

A number of the team members are enthusiastic about it. Rickie nods to the coach. "I'll be there if you're buying."

"I am," the coach says. He is relieved and happy. "All right, you guys, hit the snack stand before it closes."

"Nice game, dude," the left fielder calls to Rickie as he crosses the field toward the snack bar. Others call to him, too.

"Hey, man, good game."

"Next week the finals."

"Yeah, you, too," he calls.

Rickie stands facing the bleachers, waiting for his sister.

CHAPTER 9

You were great," Daisy says.

"What are you doing here?" Rickie says, but he doesn't mean it the way it comes out. He sees the hurt come into her eyes.

"Can't I come to see my little brother play baseball?" She brings her hand to her mouth as she speaks, a gesture she still makes unconsciously. She began doing it years ago when she had braces.

"Yeah, sure," he says, uncertain what's to happen next. She has climbed gingerly down the bleachers and now stands looking at him, holding a hand up to shield her eyes from the sun. She is about the same height as Rickie.

"C'mon. I'll take you home to change. Then we can go get something to eat. I'm starving."

He looks at her more closely as they walk across the field toward the parking lot. Her thick, wiry hair is pulled back into a ponytail, exposing her forehead and her round face. The acne has cleared up. She is wearing a little make-up. She is becoming prettier, thinner than he remembered, but her lack of confidence shows in her face and gestures. She always looks ready to bolt and run away, like a wild deer.

"What?" she asks.

"Nothing."

"You don't want to go?"

"Yeah, I do. I... I haven't seen you for a while."

"No, I know. I've been working, *mi'jo*. Going to school. I don't have much time. I'm sorry."

"It's okay. I was only saying." He doesn't want to say anything more, afraid that he will upset her. She has always been easy to bring to frustrated tears.

They get into her grey Nissan, old now, but clean. Of course she keeps it washed and vacuumed on the inside. The paint on the driver's side of the hood has flaked off in a large patch. She starts it and turns on the air conditioner.

"I don't know how you stand the heat, *mi'jo*. It's just barely eleven and I'm sweating."

"I don't really feel it."

"You must have ice inside you," she says and laughs. "Did you want to take a friend to lunch, Junior? I just got paid."

"They pay you good at your job?"

"As a teacher's aide? It's not bad because I work with Special Ed. kids, but I don't have much left over after bills every month." He glances over at her. She tightens the muscles around her mouth and looks inward, as though puzzling how to change this state of affairs. "I thought you might want to take a friend," she says, emerging from her thoughts and relaxing her facial muscles.

"No, no friends. How about your boyfriend?"

"*What* boyfriend? I haven't got time for a boyfriend." She

laughs ruefully.

They drive slowly through the residential area to their grand-mother's house.

People are still out in front of their houses finishing the morn-ing's work. Soon it will be too hot. Cars have been washed, lawns mowed and watered, yards raked and sprinkled to keep the dust down. Men lean deep into engine compartments of cars parked at the curb or disappear up to the shins beneath cars up on jacks or blocks. *Vatos* in pressed T-shirts or undershirts, some with bandanas around their foreheads or necks, stand in the dimin-ishing shade at the front of a house and raise their cans of beer to Daisy. She acknowledges them by turning her head only slightly and giving them a little smile. They call something to her, but the rolled-up windows and the air conditioner blanket the words.

"Take a shower and then we'll go. Maybe we'll get *abuelita* to go with us. Dress nice," she adds as they get out of the car.

After he has showered and dressed, he finds Daisy and their grandmother sitting at the kitchen table. Berta only works a few hours on Saturdays. The back door is open and Berta fans herself with the cardboard backing from a writing tablet. They look at him when he comes into the room. He has put on a clean white T-shirt, khaki pants, and his black Nikes.

"What happened to that nice shirt I gave you for your birth-day?" Daisy asks.

"I got it. I wear it sometimes," he lies.

"Can you wear it now? You look... like everybody else in that," she says, holding back.

"No. It needs to be ironed."

His grandmother just looks at him and says nothing.

"She's not going. It's too hot for her outside." Daisy turns to her grandmother and tells her in Spanish, "They have air-conditioning. You can get cool there." The grandmother only shakes her head. Once Daisy suggested that she get air-conditioning in the house.

"Who pays?" her grandmother asked.

The restaurant stands on a busy street corner, a little place with concrete benches and tables outside under faded green and red metal umbrellas. No matter that the owner hoses down the outside walls and tiled roof, and sweeps the wet benches and tables every evening, there is a permanent griminess to the place from the dirt and exhaust of the intersection. Inside, the restaurant has the gamy, sour odor of *menudo* and the pervasive reek of heated lard.

It is the only restaurant they go to in the neighborhood. Bill and Daisy might go to other, better places near their apartments or near college, but when they return home, they come here. They have come here as long as anyone can remember. The previous owner had been a friend of their grandfather's.

Daisy and Rickie sit inside in the cool, heavy air blown into the room by the swamp cooler. They eat without speaking for a while. Rickie eats ravenously with a flat, otherworldly look on his face, forking in the food, hardly chewing before swallowing. Daisy watches him.

"Slow down, *mi'jo*. No one's chasing you," she says.

"I'm hungry," he answers. She eats slowly, in small bites. After every bite of her taco, she wipes her mouth. When the tacos are gone, she eats her refried beans, then the rice, and then finishes her soda. She takes a stick of gum and a mirror from her purse. She tears the gum in half, placing half next to Rickie's soda. Before unwrapping her half, she holds a mirror to her mouth and inspects her teeth. She puts the mirror away, unwraps her gum, and puts it in her mouth.

Rickie finishes his meal much before her, and he watches her with her food, the mirror and the gum. Her meticulousness, her fear of being wrong or laughed at, has always driven him crazy. He wants to yell at her, to tell her it won't do any good, but he doesn't really know what he means.

She takes his tray and her own to the trash receptacle. She is wearing a white blouse, jean shorts and tennis shoes. He watches her as she walks away and back toward him. Her rear end is round and shapely in the tight jeans, and although her blouse doesn't accentuate her breasts, it doesn't hide them either.

"What?" she asks when she catches him looking at her.

"How come you don't have a boyfriend?"

"I told you. I don't have time," she says, but she blushes because he has noticed her. "Guys are...guys are stupid. No, not stupid. Immature. It's all or nothing with them. And right now. I hope you're not like that with your girlfriend."

He thinks about saying he doesn't have one. "I'm not."

"You're a...a gentleman with her?"

He laughs. "She's...she's not like you. Maybe she doesn't want me to be a gentleman."

"Oh, Junior, you could have a nice girl."

"Okay, Mom."

"Well, who's going to tell you about girls if I don't."

"I don't need you telling me about girls. I know about them."

They fall silent.

"How are you doing in school?" she asks finally. He knew she would get to this topic. She always does.

"All right."

"C'mon, Junior. What does that mean? Are you passing everything?"

"Yeah."

"Are you getting along with your teachers?"

"Yeah. No problems."

Rickie can tell she's getting frustrated with him, but she presses on with her attempts to guide him.

"People like us, Junior, no one wants us here. If we aren't working in the fields or in the sweatshops downtown or doing day labor like our grandparents, they don't want us."

"*Abuelito* talked with you, too, didn't he?" he interrupts.

"Yes, he did. But listen for a minute," she says, a little deflated but clearly feeling her role as a big sister and surrogate mother intensely today.

"You're what? Seventeen? And almost a man. You've changed, grown more serious. It's important that you understand."

Rickie doesn't speak. He is trying not to grow impatient with her lecture.

"What is *abuelita* going to live on when she gets too old to work? She has a little saved up, but no Social Security, no pension. Who's going to care about her? The people she works for? Not a chance. They'll just get someone else."

Rickie lets his eyes wander as she talks. First he reads the menu above the order window. It has been painted on the wall in black ornamental writing against a white background. Red and green vines, with *chiles* of the opposite color dangling from them, encircle the writing. A beautiful *señorita* with long black hair and in a traditional long dress with red and green piping dances gaily as she holds a sombrero above her head. A *señor* sleeps with his head on his knees against an adobe wall. A sleepy burro and a saguaro cactus stand off to the side.

Rickie's attention is drawn to a fly buzzing in the corner of the window. He takes a napkin and traps it, pinches it until he feels its body pop. He drops the napkin on the table. Daisy falls silent before taking the napkin gingerly by one corner and throwing it away in the trash. The two men sitting across from them watch her. One shrugs and nods his approval of her to his friend.

"Junior," she says quietly after she sits down again, "you don't want to end up on the street or with your homeboys just hanging out." "Homeboys" sounds like it doesn't fit her mouth right, and he smiles. She passes it off and continues. "You've got to get your education, a college degree or something that will give you a good job. You've got to show them that you're worth something. Even so, it's going to be hard." This last statement she says almost under her breath, as though speaking to herself.

While she speaks, she leans forward with her hands flat on the table. Her earnestness makes him smile, but if she keeps it up, as she often does, he will grow tired of it and irritated.

"Do you study this stuff in college?" he asks.

"What stuff?"

"About what people think of us. About...us. Mexicans and stuff."

"Yes, I took a class called Chicano Studies. We had to read books and talk about issues in class. Sometimes it got pretty wild. For a while I joined a political group, but I quit going to the meetings after a while."

"How come you quit?"

"They had problems with women. With validating...with making women feel important or even equal. I got tired of fighting with them."

After a moment she says, "You get my point, right? They never wanted us to stay here and they still don't. The only way to win is get your education."

"I know," he says. He is ready to leave, but because she makes no movement at all when he pushes back his chair, he knows she has something else to tell him.

"I get scared sometimes," she says and looks out the window as though the source of her fear resides out there. At that moment, a mangy dog lopes by with its tongue out. It does not hesitate to cross the street, as if some destination still far off calls insistently. Traffic is light. An old pickup loaded with a rusty water heater, a washing machine and other metal to be recycled, swerves to avoid the dog. Daisy inhales noisily as she watches the dog stop just long enough not to be hit and then move on. Three men are crowded inside the pickup. The one riding shotgun yells at the dog and laughs loudly.

Daisy looks back at Rickie. "Do you ever get scared?"

"Of what? Of being hit by a car?"

"Don't joke. I'm trying to tell you something serious," she says looking down at her hands on the table. "Not of being hit by a car. It's just that sometimes I feel very alone. I wish I had someone. Not a boyfriend or a husband, just someone to turn to, to hold me and tell me that everything's gonna be okay, to take over when I get tired. Like a mom." She looks up at him. "Maybe you're not like me," she says, resigned to that possibility. She sits quietly for a while, building up courage to say what she is going to say next.

"I found my father. I've been writing to him."

Rickie doesn't understand. He stares at her uncomprehendingly for a moment.

"*Our* father. Ricardo."

It's like a punch to the abdomen.

"Why? Why would you do that? Because you're scared?"

"No, not that. I don't know. Maybe. Because I needed to. I wanted to find him. I don't even know what country my mom lives in."

"How did you find him?" Rickie is still astounded and stalling for time to process this new information.

"Last year I began to call all the Ricardo Trujillos and R. Trujillos up that way—Thousand Oaks, Camarillo, Oxnard, Ventura. Do you know how many there are? More than a hundred! He's up in Ventura." She pauses, excited now that she has begun to tell him. He will allow no reaction to show on his face. He has never talked to her about their father; they don't talk about their past at all, Bill included. Bill's anger still remains on the surface. He dismisses their father and mother as ignorant Mexicans who only care about themselves.

"When someone actually answered, I told them I wanted to speak to Ricardo Trujillo. A lot of times they'd hang up or say that no Ricardo Trujillo lived there. But this one time, a man answered and said, 'Who is this?' I told him I was Daisy, Ricardo's daughter. He didn't say anything for a long time, didn't hang up and didn't say he didn't have a daughter, either. It was like he was deciding whether to admit who he was or not. Finally, he said, 'How old are you now?' I told him. He said, 'What about Bill and Junior?' and then I knew for sure."

She stops. Rickie is looking at her intently, trying to understand what renewed contact with their father means to his life. Daisy looks down at her hands folded in front of her, then takes a napkin from the holder and polishes the space on the table in front of her.

"You probably think I'm stupid for calling him," she says without looking up.

"I don't care what you do. It's your life. What did you tell him about me?"

"That you were okay."

"That's all?"

"No, a little more. What should I have said?"

"Nothing. I don't want him to know nothing about me. What else did you say?"

"I wrote him a long letter after he gave me his post office box number. I sat at the kitchen table the next night and told him about me, about Bill, about you and about *abuelita*…"

"What did you say about me?" he asks. Suddenly, the food he has eaten is making him ill.

"I only told him a little bit—about what grade you're in… I told him you were doing well. Are you? I hope so."

Rickie doesn't respond.

"About baseball. About your arrest… I had to, Junior," she says when he is about to object. "I wanted to be honest. I told him I worried about your friends. But I told him how good you are in baseball, that he'd be proud."

Rickie stares at her and shakes his head back and forth slowly as though he can't believe what she has done.

She pushes on. "I told him you didn't have anyone, that we had our grandfather after he left, but that *abuelito's* gone and our grandmother is old and worn out, and she doesn't really understand how things are."

Rickie is too shaken to respond; he searches her face to try to understand why she has brought this stranger back into their lives.

"After I was sure he had received the letter, I called again. We talked for over an hour. He cried, Junior. He was very ashamed. He cried like a baby."

The expression on Rickie's face remains impassive, but he can feel something begin to constrict within him, as though it will eventually choke him.

"Do you call him a lot?" he asks.

"He wants me to, but I write him more. It takes my mind off things, gives me something to do."

"I thought you didn't have time for anything besides work and school," he says. His tone is accusatory.

"He's our father, Junior. I'm going to make time to write him. Besides, when I don't have school at night, I have too much time. It's not like I have this wild social life. I don't even have a boyfriend, remember?" Self-pity has found its way into her voice.

He feels the grip tighten. He wants to think that his sister is always moving forward, not alone, and not lonely and trying to grasp at something from the past. He knows so little about her. Even when he was quite young, he distanced himself from her because she bossed him around too much. He has always been willing to concede that she knows how things ought to be, how he ought to act, but he often resists her direction. She gives the people who make the rules too much power. She follows the letter of the law too perfectly and shrinks back in disbelief and fear if someone, Rickie or one of his friends, breaks the law or any of those unwritten laws she believes in. It is as though she knows something he does not, that some black-hooded punisher hides in the shadows and waits to hand out harsh justice if you break a law.

"He won't help," he says bitterly.

"What?"

"He won't help if you're scared. He wasn't there when we were little kids afraid of little kid stuff. He couldn't handle that. What makes you think he can help now? He doesn't give a shit about us. If he did, he'd of shown up years ago. He knows where we are. We haven't moved," he says dismissively. "Is he still with that fourteen-year-old?"

"She's not fourteen any longer, Junior. That was years ago. No, he's not. He feels ashamed. He doesn't come back because he is ashamed of everything he did. He told me over and over." She pauses. She can tell that he doesn't believe her or doesn't care. "He always asks about you, Junior, wants to know about your baseball. He wants to see you play."

"The season's almost over. There's only the championship game. He'll have to get his sorry ass down here quick," he says quietly, but she hears him.

"Junior."

"Does Bill know?" he asks, ignoring her scolding look.

"I told him, but he doesn't care. 'He's out of my life,' he says. What about you, Junior? What do you think?"

"I think he should stay up there with his fourteen-year-old," he says and stands to leave.

Daisy looks as if she's going to correct him but thinks better of it. She takes a napkin from the dispenser and pushes the gum out of her mouth into it. She balls up the napkin and throws it away in the trash as they exit. In the parking lot, the afternoon heat engulfs them from all sides. It feels as though cool air has never existed and never will again, only hot, still air; as though they are inside a balloon filled with poisonous gas. He takes the gum from his mouth and throws it into the bushes.

They go inside the house. Their grandmother is stretched out on the sofa, TV on, fan on and directed at her. She sleeps on her back in her dark blue dress, her mostly toothless mouth open and taking in air noisily.

They both stare at her for a long moment, pity and love registering on Daisy's face. She reaches out her hand to smooth the hair away from her grandmother's forehead but holds back.

"Okay, I don't want to wake her up. I'm going to go." She leans over and kisses Rickie on the cheek. He stands rigidly. "I'll come see you play next week. That's the championship game, right? Maybe Billy, too. I'll call him."

He watches her get in her car and drive off. In this unguarded moment he feels a wave of sadness and regret and anger sweep over him. She is good, she cares about him, but the image of her driving away in her grey car with its front bumper dimpled from some parking lot mishap and the paint peeled off the hood, makes her seem small and vulnerable. They are alone, even if she calls that bastard and writes him. It isn't other people—the whites or blacks or Chinese or whomever she means when she says other people don't want them here. Those people aren't the problem. Their own father and mother are the problem. *They* didn't want them, not then, not now. Has Daisy forgotten that? She and Bill and Rickie didn't walk out on their parents. Their parents abandoned them, he for his fourteen-year-old, and she for some broken-down biker.

One time, one time only, Rickie remembers his father taking him to Toys "R" Us to buy him something. Even as young as he was, Rickie knew it had nothing to do with a father's love; the boy was being bought off in an attempt by the father to buy his way out of the guilt for not attending Rickie's kindergarten or first grade class to ooh and aah over a stupid folder of his work or the performance of some simple-minded song. His father tried to make a big deal of the trip to the toy store, but Rickie was determined not to give him an easy out. He refused to pick a toy, choosing instead to stand by the cash registers looking at batteries. His father picked out a cheap yellow plastic squirt gun, which Rickie took out back when they got home and smashed by stomping on it without even taking it off the card. He didn't bother to pick up the mess. His father never asked him about it.

Every now and then when he sat with his mother on the couch to watch TV, she drew him close to her and held him tightly, but she never spoke when she hugged him, just held him tightly as though she wanted to squeeze the life out of him.

She was Rickie's age when she got married; she didn't know anything about the world outside the neighborhood. She was a poor student, didn't finish high school, so she did what other girls do who feel unimportant and without a future: she got pregnant and had a baby, had three babies, and later on, still feeling worthless, she married a fat, mean loser who rode a motorcycle and beat her and gave her more babies. To Rickie, she is just another pathetic victim, remote and unforgivable.

CHAPTER 10

Rickie sits on the end of his bed and faces his dresser with his trophies and the mirror behind them, but he doesn't look at the trophies or the reflection of himself in the mirror. He stares at the nondescript, flattened carpet, aware that time stretches before him like an endless, empty desert. He tries to bring to mind the morning's game and his sister and the fact that she is writing to their father. The game has already receded into that place of forgotten things, like a TV show that he has just watched, whose details he cannot recall. He tries to force the game to take on the significance of games in the past, about which he used to be able to remember each play and each at-bat in detail; be able to re-play them in his head with the clarity of a film clip. But this most recent game refuses to come forward into the present. He can't bring it back vividly. Worse than that, he realizes that it doesn't really matter.

Daisy. Did she just take him to lunch to tell him that she is writing to their father? Rickie didn't have to know, doesn't want to know anything about that man. But why *did* she write him? What was her real reason? Was it because she's lonely? She must be. Even though he can admit to himself that he is sometimes desperately lonely and feels as though he is an alien with little connection to the other inhabitants of the planet, and even though he sometimes feels a need for guidance, and in the still of the night feels a sob well up within him like the cry of some wild animal, he will not reach out or in any way show himself to this low-life who walked out on them because he was too hot to screw some fourteen-year-old to care about his own children. Rickie will never write him or talk to him. Never. Not to their mother, either. They are the past. Dead.

"Smile now, cry later," the saying goes. He sees it tattooed on the biceps of *veteranos* and the forearms of *veteranas* in a banner below the masks of comedy and tragedy. But that won't be his motto. His will be, "Cry yesterday, laugh today." He cried all he is going to cry years ago when they left. He cried until he emptied himself of tears and sound and vision and feeling. He learned how not to be present, to disappear behind flat, vacant eyes so that he feels nothing, and if something has the potential to bother him, to penetrate his outside wall, it will find only an echoing tunnel inside him. He has become a shark, the name they gave him, with no feelings whatsoever, just purpose.

It has taken a while. He suffered the ministrations of elementary school teachers who discovered him crying at his table. His tablemate would proudly shoot a hand high in the air. "*Maestra*, Rickie is crying," she would call out. "I think he misses his mom again," she would say with the smug certainty of little girls.

The teachers took him aside and gave him tissues and wiped

his nose. They held him to them and stroked his head or patted him. And when his classmates found him standing by himself on the playground at recess, they came up to him, the little girls mothering like the teacher. "What's wrong, Rickie? Are you sad about your mom?" they asked and stroked his skinny arm. The boys, except for his best friend, Alex, stood off a bit. "C'mon, Rickie, run with us. We're going to jump over the benches by Miss Peterson's room." They were so sure that running and jumping or playing tetherball or kickball would cure the hurt. Alex put his arm around him and comforted him and walked with him to the benches. At the end of recess, the others ran up to the teacher and told her with earnest faces that Rickie had been thinking about his mom and dad again. Teacher shook her pretty head sadly.

With the exception of Alex, they all, teachers and classmates alike, receded into an anonymous group he has trouble remembering as individuals. Yes, the students went on just as he had into middle school and high school, but he grew so distant from the child he had been.

Only if someone, a girl usually, brought out a class photo from one of those elementary school years—of twenty-five beaming little boys and girls and a young, harried teacher standing primly at one end—and pointed to herself and then pointed to Rickie seated cross-legged on the floor or standing in the back row with a wan smile on his face, only then did he remember the faces and who they were. Rickie would look at the person standing next to him and back at the picture and finally make the connection, as though he were just waking from sleep.

At first, during the middle school years, the others looked at him occasionally as though they remembered his hard times and had questions, but they did not speak. Quickly enough, they forgot his troubles to focus on their own. Only Alex speaks to him these days about the past, but Rickie usually cuts him off before it goes too far.

"Why do you want to remember those days, fool?" Rickie asks. "They're dead. I don't think about them."

He sits without moving for a long time and becomes aware of the tightness in his shoulders. Probably from the game. Worse than that is the cramping anxiety in his stomach. He knows its cause. He has to do something, prove something to somebody. Stupid Oscar. He shouldn't have to prove anything to anybody. Sharks never have to establish purpose; it is there at the moment of birth. The shark doesn't think about what it's doing and it doesn't feel remorse or happiness; it is a killing machine because that is just what it is born to be.

He wants to join the Marines in a couple of years. He wants some hardass D.I. to yell and work him to the point of exhaustion and empty him of every question or doubt or feeling. Then he will be lean, bright, hard and able to kill without question or thought.

He looks around his room again and feels no more interest in it than he had the day before. Maybe he should clear the dresser, put the trophies, hats, newspaper clippings, and signed baseballs all in boxes. His Xbox—what should he do with it? He has only played once recently. Alex came over. They smoked a joint and laughed as terrorists were killed, cars crashed, snowboarders somersaulted off mountains and tumbled into deep ravines, and idiots fell off floating platforms into the abyss. But it all grew old quickly. Their laughter rang hollow. They quit in the middle of the game, at a loss as to what to do next. Alex went home soon afterwards and Rickie slept. He tries to sleep more and more these days.

A pile of magazines sits on the floor by the TV—*Black Belts* and *Lowriders* and a *Playboy*. He bought the *Black Belt* magazines thinking he would learn some of the moves described in them. He and Alex made a couple of attempts to mimic the photographs frame by frame, but they became self-conscious when so many of the moves entailed grabbing one another's hand or wrist or shirt front or pinning one another on the floor. They tried to laugh it off—"Hey, faggot, let go of my hand!" Eventually they quit trying the moves after a few more embarrassed attempts.

He picks up a copy of *Lowrider*. He doesn't care about the amateurish photos of shirtless *vatos* and bikini-clad *jainas* standing next to polished Buicks and Oldsmobiles and Chevys rearing up on their hydraulics. It's the drawings of the *chicanos* and *chicanas* who are ideals of *la raza*. The men are drawn with thick mustaches, flat stomachs, bandanas and tattoos, and the women are impossibly slim and busty. Both men and women have large dark eyes full of passion and despair. They have thick, black, straight hair, shiny and swept back. His hair has never been straight. Wavy and thick, it was an unmanageable mass, no matter how much Three Flowers he put in it to hold it in place.

After taking the car, he shaved his head. His grandmother was horrified and told him that he looked like the photographs of criminals she saw in the newspapers left on the kitchen tables of the houses she cleaned.

"What do you know, *abuelita*?" he asked dismissively. After all, she is an old lady who understands nothing.

"They are in gangs, they steal cars, they kill people. You can see in their eyes that they are no good."

"I'm not a criminal. I don't kill nobody. It's just the style now."

"To look like a criminal? I don't understand." She shook her head in dismay. The lines seemed to deepen on her dark face. She reached out and touched the black stubble on his head and pulled her hand back quickly.

"It's no good," she said and turned away from him.

Rickie turns on the fan and lies back on his bed. The moving air comforts him, and he falls asleep easily. His facial muscles relax, the hardened face softens,

He dreams. *He is in the field in his usual position near second base. Someone is yelling in his face, too close to distinguish the features—is it the coach, his father, some male teacher? Whoever it is, he is yelling at Rickie to cover second, a runner is coming. No runner is in sight or any other players on his own team, but he hears footsteps pounding down the base path, not fast, but heavy. He knows if he turns his head completely to his left, he will see the runner bearing down on him, but he doesn't. Instead, he watches the face of the man in front of him, which he finally recognizes as Maltrey's face. He is furious, yelling at Rickie, spit spraying from his mouth. Rickie watches him impassively, both of them knowing that Maltrey cannot touch him, and that knowledge only increases Maltrey's frustrated rage. Rickie would have been smugly amused by it, except that the sound of the footsteps of the advancing runner is relentless and steady. The runner has to be huge, has to be nearly on top of him, and Rickie hasn't made a move toward second base. Now when he tries to, his legs are too heavy to lift. It, whatever it is, comes on and on...*

He wakes up with a sharp jerk of his legs and lies still on the bed as the dream slowly dissolves in the afternoon light. The fan provides a steady and comforting stream of air and sound. In the near distance, he hears the tailing-off roar of one of the corporate jets booming out of the airport.

He sits up on the edge of the bed and wonders how much time has passed. A few minutes? An hour? He leans over and raises the yellowed shade to check the afternoon sky. The light is white and blinding.

He gets up and goes through the kitchen deep in afternoon stillness. In the living room his grandmother still lies on the couch asleep. Her mouth is open, her brown wrinkled hands crossed at her stomach. He pauses and looks hard at her open mouth and chest to make sure she is breathing. At that moment, she takes in a deep breath with a snore. He smiles then, amused by the cartoonish noise of the snore.

Her once black hair, which she used to brush until it shone, now lies in a grey mass under her head. Dark veins map her legs. The skin on her forearms has become papery dry and thin, easily bruised. Calluses dot her lined hands where fingers meet the palm. And the fingers themselves are knobby and bent. She massages them constantly, soaks them in basins of warm water, sometimes in ice water to reduce the swelling.

She seems too fragile, too brittle to work as she does. How long can she keep it up? What will happen to him if she can't work? Where will he go? Who will he live with?

He shouldn't have to worry, he thinks. None of this is his fault. He never asked for parents to abandon him, a grandfather to die too soon, a grandmother to grow old in just a few years... He hadn't asked to live.

But when he looks at her face to find a place to lay his anger, he cannot find it. What wells up inside of him at that moment of looking at her small, worn body he chokes back. He turns away from her and goes into the kitchen to call Alex.

SATURDAY AFTERNOON

CHAPTER 11

Rickie and Alex are on their way to Wendy's house when they are spotted by a carload of 18th Street gang members.

On the south side of Sycamore Way there are two or three small street gangs and a handful of crews like the one Rickie and Alex formed; the north side of the boulevard and beyond belongs to 18th Street. There are a few tagging crews as well, but they tag well out of the immediate area. Everyone on both sides of the line lives in an edgy truce. If you don't go on certain streets at certain times of the day; if you stay on your own blocks and on the established routes to the schools or the stores or on the main streets during daylight hours, you're all right. Only occasionally does someone violate the unspoken agreement.

If an upstart gang suddenly appears, news travels through the neighborhood and everyone waits for the inevitable result: one night someone gets jumped and badly beaten; a drive-by occurs on Vineyard; or someone is shot and killed as he sits at a light on

Glen Ellen on his way home from work. The new gang, all studied stances and unforgiving expressions even the night before, is dispersed by morning. No one speaks of it. No one claims it. All that remains are the tags on cinderblock walls, dumpsters and back lot windows, markings whose reference quickly becomes obscure and so unimportant that no one even bothers to cross them out.

Wendy lives in the neighborhood claimed by 18th Street. It is almost 5:00 o'clock that Saturday afternoon. The heat is beginning to drain from the day. Streets are quiet. Everyone is inside in air-conditioned rooms or sitting in front of fans or sitting outside under shade trees. Tonight, perhaps, it will cool down.

Rickie and Alex stay on Landerman, one of the main boulevards heading north, for as long as they can, but they have to cut west into the neighborhood to get to Wendy's house. They walk quickly now. No breeze stirs. If they stop to listen, they will be struck by the quiet. No jets take off. No music blares from someone's backyard. No kids play in front yards and no dogs bark. A few cars pass slowly. The boys eye their occupants surreptitiously; open staring or prolonged eye contact might provoke an angry outburst—arms open, palms up, head thrown back in a threatening shrug: "What the fuck're you looking at?" And then who knows what might happen?

Rickie sees the old black Camry as he and Alex are about to cross the intersection to Wendy's block. The car is pulled up to the curb in front of her house facing them. Quickly, hoping it's not obvious what they are doing, Rickie leans on Alex and forces him to keep walking straight.

"What?"

"Eighteenth," Rickie says under his breath. "On the right. In front of Wendy's. Don't look," he says, but it makes no difference.

They have been noticed. They walk past Wendy's street, still heading west. The car pulls away from the curb and turns onto the street where the boys are walking. The car creeps along on the wrong side of the street, parallel and close to the boys. There are no cars parked on this side of the street, nothing between the boys and this car full of *vatos*.

"Hey, pussies, where're you from?" the driver asks, leaning out the open window. His short black hair is greased and in a net. Rickie and Alex don't answer. Nor do they turn their heads. Rickie, who walks on the curbside of the sidewalk, glances without turning his head at the driver and at the open window in back. There are two people in front; there might be three people in the back. The windows are black with heavy tint.

"Hey, I'm talking to you girls. Where're you from, I said?"

An old Toyota pickup turns onto the street and heads toward them. Lawn mowers and gardening tools are loaded in the back, two men crowded in the front. As they near the Camry and realize the situation, they swerve into the other lane and go around. Rickie glances back hopefully and sees the driver's and the passenger's faces in the side mirrors as they drive off.

"Not talking?" he says, addressing Rickie. "Must mean you're in the wrong 'hood. That's too bad." He turns away and speaks to the others in a low voice. Everyone laughs.

At the moment that he sees the back window go all the way down and the dull black barrel of the pistol appear on the edge of the rear window, Rickie becomes aware of the whole neighborhood. It is as though he has the ability to take a full 360-degree view with all of his senses. He is struck by how empty, how still everything is. With the exception of the truck disappearing in the opposite direction, nothing moves. No one comes out of a house on his or her way somewhere. No bird flies from tree to tree. No breeze stirs the leaves already flagging in the late spring heat. Where is anybody? It's as though everyone and everything knows what this moment portends and has decided to hold its collective breath and let it happen. They are alone. No one will step in.

Rickie throws out his left hand, catching Alex in the stomach.

"Run!" he commands.

They stop dead in their tracks and run back diagonally across a poor yard toward a white wooden gate, expecting at any moment to feel that searing pain in the back of a leg, or in the back or neck, or the red explosion in their heads. It is a dirt yard, swept and watered that afternoon. The gate on the far side of the house that leads into the back yard is painted white and made of wood, the paint peeling and the wood weather-beaten. They will get splinters in their hands when they vault it. There will be that moment when they'll be at the top, a moment when they are no longer ascending and not yet descending, when each of them will be frozen mid-arc, when they will be easy targets. Rickie can imagine the laughter as the bullets rip into his back, the horrible pain, the blackness or, worse yet, waking up in a hospital to find himself with no feeling below the waist because his spine has been severed, condemned for the rest of his life to be bound to a wheelchair, fed by others, ass wiped by others, slobbering from the corner of his mouth...

Rivulets of cold sweat run from Rickie's armpits down his sides. He reaches for the top of the gate and pulls himself up as hard as he can.

Have shots already been fired? Has there already been the rapid loud popping of a nine-millimeter? He can't hear well because his heart is like the ocean in his ears.

He jumps the gate in a bound, falls awkwardly on the concrete, hitting his knee hard. He watches Alex scrabble over the gate, balance for a moment and jump down. This time he hears the bullet hit a board a few inches from the top just as Alex clears it and falls on his shoulder. The piece of the board snapped off by the bullet hits Alex in the side of the head.

"Shit," he cries, snatching at the right side of his head. He pulls his hand away and stares at it, surprised that he finds no blood. He rubs the shoulder he landed on.

The car screeches around the corner. The chase is going to continue.

"Back over," Rickie calls. Alex doesn't get it. "Jump back over. They're coming around the back. Quick!"

The owner of the house, unshaven and bleary-eyed, in black shorts and an unbuttoned white shirt, stands up uncertainly from the folding chair where he has fallen asleep and comes toward them. A pit bull snarls and jumps behind a flimsy screen door.

"You goddam kids! ¡*Hijos de la chingada*! Get outta here. You ruin everything with your gangs and tagging and drive-bys. Get out before I let the dog on you!"

The dog jumps hard at the screen door. Rickie looks from the dog to the man's face. His thick black hair is an uncombed mess, and his eyes are dark and bloodshot. A heavy black mustache covers his upper lip. Rickie sees the fear in the man's eyes for the family he has hidden in the house, for his black Nissan parked in the driveway, for his neatly kept front and backyards, and his dusty pink and blue hydrangeas planted next to the front steps. In the tick of a second it takes to register all of this, Rickie feels a surge of anger and despair and a desire to lash out at this man and his stupid dog and whoever has made life this way.

They vault back onto the driveway.

"Which way?" Alex calls, out of breath, rubbing his sore shoulder.

"Cross."

They run across the street, looking for a place into which they can disappear. Every house on this side is too visible from either end of the street. Each has a tall gate leading into the back-yard with who knows what behind it—a Rottweiler, a pit bull, a German Shepherd.

They run down the block toward Landerman Boulevard. They can see people crossing the street and a stream of cars go-ing each way, a friendly sight but seemingly a galaxy away. Here, as their footsteps pound on the broken and raised concrete of the sidewalk, there is that stillness again, that eerie quiet as though the world in this neighborhood, on this block, has stopped spin-ning and everything but the two of them and the car of gangsters has suspended all activity, all motion.

The car is getting too close. The boys heave into the alley that runs in back of Landerman. When they are halfway down the block, the Camry noses into the alley, too. They have to decide again. Go left, back into the neighborhood, or right, out to the boulevard where it will be safe.

"Head for the street," Rickie yells as he hears the Camry speed up in back of them. But right here there are no breaks in the back walls of the stores that line the boulevard. They try a few doors, but the alley doors are locked. Rickie's lungs burn, his legs are tired and getting clumsy. He knows that the least little thing, a hump in the asphalt, a pothole, some piece of trash that gets tangled in his feet, will bring him to his knees.

Suddenly he sees a metal gate open into someone's backyard. He runs left. Alex follows him and slams the gate behind him. It swings open again as the car passes slowly. The gangsters can see the open gate, and they know where Rickie and Alex have gone.

The boys step and hop their way gingerly past the overturned barbecue kettle, the rusting tricycle, the garden tools scattered about, and the exploded mattresses spewing their insides out on the driveway concrete. The screen for the sliding glass doors is torn and leaning against the wall. A hole has been smashed in the brittle siding of the wall next to the back door, revealing a stud and some wiring. They head for the gate that leads into the front yard.

They hear the car squeal in reverse, still in the alley. Good, Rickie thinks: they have a minute or two. They kick the gate open into the front yard.

They look up and down the quiet street. In the background, they hear tires squeal again; the car will be leaving the alley and coming around the corner. They need to move quickly.

Down the block and across the street a small house sits beneath the deep shade of a tree in full early leaf. The house is old, single story and in an old style. The burgundy paint on the outside walls and the black paint on the ornamental shutters have both faded from years of neglect. Rickie's grandfather would have something to tell Rickie about it if he were still alive.

They cross the street and sprint through the yard past a For Sale sign lying on its back in the brown and overgrown grass. Just then the Camry turns the corner. Alex and Rickie crouch down and duck-walk as quickly as they can along the driveway toward the back of the vacant house. Broken glass lies scattered beneath a side window. They stand up straight, backs against the side of the house near the glinting pile of glass. Rickie puts his arm out against Alex's heaving chest, backing him closer to the house.

"Quiet, fool," he whispers. "Shit, you're breathing hard enough to be heard in Pacoima! C'mon," he says. "Let's try to get in."

"No. If they figure it out, we'll be trapped in there. I'm going to go watch for them. Look for a way out."

"We'll just jump the back wall." Neither of them moves for a moment; they are bent over now, with their hands on their knees, breathing deeply to slow their pounding hearts.

"Look for dogs," Alex heaves. "I hate dogs."

Alex leans out away from the side of the house to view the street. Rickie goes around the side of the garage to the back wall and peers into the neighbor's yard. The neighbor's climbing rose bush and bougainvillea with its long thorns back up against this wall; the boys have to hope they won't need to exit this way.

"Hey," Rickie calls quietly, but loud enough to be heard by a dog in the yard. "Hey," he calls again. No dog.

He turns and sees Alex squatting low and leaning over to view the street. He also sees that the back door is open.

"Alex."

"I think they drove by," Alex says in a low voice. "But we better wait."

Rickie joins him. They listen and watch for the car for five minutes more. Their breathing quiets.

"C'mon, they're gone," Rickie says. He continues to speak in a low voice. "Let's check this place out. The back door is wide open."

Alex leaves his position reluctantly, looking back frequently as they walk around to the back of the house.

The yard is neat, empty of the junk that had been in the yard of the other place. The garage door is closed. To the left of the garage there is a little plot of grass. Fuchsias, ferns and Birds of Paradise have been planted in a narrow strip along the garage wall and along the tall metal fencing that divides this yard from the neighbors in back. Someone once worked hard to create this little oasis back here, but it has been abandoned to become rank and overgrown. A tall avocado tree shades the yard and the back steps.

Inside, the place is bare and clean except for shards of window glass on the kitchen floor and in the sink. Next in line to the kitchen on the way to the front of the house is a dining room with built-in glass-fronted cabinets. Beyond it is the living room. A large mirror or painting once covered most of one wall. Where it hung, there is now a large rectangle of brighter yellow paint. Someone has tagged inside that space with black spray paint. It is inexpert and unpracticed. The boys stand in front of it and view it critically.

"Do you have anything on you?" Rickie finally asks. "We've got to cross this fool out. This is nasty," he adds as he inspects the tag close up.

"Not for that mess. But check this out," Alex says. He produces a can of Glade air freshener.

"Where'd you get that?" Rickie asks with surprise.

"It was right here. On the floor." He points to the wall in back of them.

"Spray it one time."

Alex sprays the air freshener and the room is filled with a heavy floral scent. Rickie nods his head in approval. "Old school. Do you remember by the handball courts in 7th grade? We got fucked up on this shit."

"And check this out," he says, pulling a joint wrapped up in a plastic sandwich bag from his front shirt pocket.

Rickie stares at him with admiration. "Fire it up!"

They sit down with their backs against the bare wall and smoke the joint hungrily, pulling on it until the ember glows long and bright orange, inhaling the burning smoke deeply. In between hits they spray the air freshener into their mouths and inhale it. The heavily scented aerosol makes Rickie gag and retch as he huffs it, but he lets himself be pulled willingly into the black whirlpool as his limbs grow heavier and heavier with every inhalation. It is as though the air itself has taken on mass and weight, has become palpable and focused right above him, pushing him down and immobilizing him. Soon it will flatten him onto the floor, but he worries no more about that than he worries about the gangsters finding them. He knows he will not be able to claw his way back to mobility if they burst in through the back door. He can't even stand, much less defend himself. But when he considers this, he discovers that he doesn't care. Let them find him. Let them kill him. Death can only be a sweet deepening of this.

He looks over at Alex. His eyes are half closed and twitching. He is slumped awkwardly against the wall ready to slip over on his side. Rickie does nothing to straighten him. The can of Glade rests on Alex's stomach. Rickie feels the pall of darkness growing around him and wonders briefly before he passes out if they are going to die here. He doesn't care as long as it doesn't hurt.

CHAPTER 12

When they wake up, the room is cast in darkness. Rickie's left arm is without feeling, and he wonders groggily if it has died already and if death is moving slowly through his body. He can't remember where they are, nor does he have any idea what time it is. His chest aches as though bound with tight bands; it is thick with disgusting stuff he will have to cough up and spit out. When his eyes focus, he finds Alex's head resting on his left shoulder. That's why I can't feel it, he thinks, and shoulders him roughly away. Alex sags over on his left side and moans. Rickie massages his arm until feeling begins to return.

"Wake up," he says, pushing Alex with his hand. Alex moans again. "C'mon, fool, wake up. It's dark. I feel like shit. I don't know if I can stand up." He braces one hand on his friend's shoulder and pushes himself up the wall, shoving Alex to the floor as he does so. His head lies at an awkward angle. Rickie leans against the wall until the dizziness and nausea lessen. He listens to the darkness, scared now, holds his breath. There is no sound—no creak or shuffle or pop—as though the house holds its breath as well. Outside, he can hear music from a party.

"C'mon, let's get out of here, " Rickie says in a low voice. He wants to get outside quickly now, his fear of being trapped in the house growing steadily.

Alex turns so that he's on his hands and knees. He coughs until he chokes and gags, drool and snot issuing from his mouth and nose. He wipes his face with his T-shirt, not moving from his hands and knees until he catches his breath.

"Jesus Christ," he says in a low, hoarse voice. "Help me up."

Rickie reaches down and grabs his hand and elbow and heaves him to his feet. Alex, too, stands with his back against the wall, breathing heavily, rubbing his face with his hand.

Carefully, they pick their way through the shadowed rooms of the house to the back door and outside. The air is still and warm, heavy with the day's smog. The sound of the band is much clearer now. Trumpets and violins and guitars, an accordion and a male voice and a female voice—it's mariachi. The boys head toward the house and the music.

Walking helps them clear their heads, both of them hacking and coughing and spitting the thickness that fills their chests. Rickie's head pounds.

"What are you going to do?" Alex asks.

"We showed those *pendejos*, didn't we?" Rickie says, walking along jauntily now.

"Who?"

"Whoever. Those gangsters."

"Yeah. So? We're just lucky we found that place."

Rickie looks at him disdainfully. "Dude, nobody can touch us."

"Yeah, right. Where're you going?"

"To check out this party."

"What if it's them?"

"Then we don't go. Let's just check it out."

They reach the end of the street. Across from where they stand, behind tall black wrought iron fencing and gates, lies a deep and wide front yard leading up to a two-story house. The size of the house and its expanse of well-kept yard make it an anomaly in this neighborhood.

"The mariachi. This place. Dude, this *cabron* has money," Alex says in wonderment.

"Must be a dealer or a lawyer or something," Rickie says.

The boys cross the street and look in at the fence; they stand about fifty feet down from the gate where two security guards wearing tight black pants and tight black T-shirts check everyone who comes in or goes out. They also keep a wary eye on anyone who drives by. Rickie knows there are others walking around inside and probably some in a car nearby. The security people at the gate have nightsticks and radios; maybe those in the car have guns. As long as no shots are fired, the cops who drive slowly past every half-hour don't stop and don't ask any questions. It's better to let these people control their own.

Strands of white Christmas lights are strung in the trees and from tree to tree throughout the front yard. More than twenty long tables covered with white tablecloths sit beneath the trees. Candles flicker at each table. Close to the house the band is set up on a makeshift stage.

"It's someone's wedding. We probably know them. C'mon, let's check it out," Rickie says.

"How're you going to get in there? You're playing with fire, fool. We don't belong here."

"It's a party. There's food. Fine-looking girls. Who knows what might happen. Aren't you hungry? As long as we don't make trouble, we'll be all right. C'mon, don't be a pussy."

"I can't. Look at me." Alex's T-shirt is rumpled and dirty from wiping his nose and mouth. Rickie looks at his own outfit, pulls on the bottom of the shirt to straighten it. Because they were headed to Wendy's house originally and he always wants to look good for girls, Rickie wore a collarless buttoned black shirt and black pants. In the dark they look dressy.

"No one will see. Turn your shirt inside out."

They grip the bars of the fence above their heads and peer in, hoping to catch sight of someone they know. Most people, the ones walking nearby or sitting languidly at the tables, are in shadow. The boys only see faces when people cross through the lighted area near the house, but then it's at a distance. The men and boys in the wedding party have shed their jackets and parade around in their white, heavily ruffled tuxedo shirts and shiny black pants. The women and girls of the wedding party wear lavender gowns with low-cut bodices. Everyone else is dressed as people usually dress for these weddings—in suits or frilly dresses, some in pressed T-shirts or blouses and jeans or black pressed pants.

"C'mon, let's try it."

"No, dude, I ain't dressed right. And I don't feel too good. I'm going home. I'll eat at home."

Rickie looks over at him, trying to decipher his real reason for not wanting to go in. Alex continues to hold onto the bars but looks down as he kicks the grass at his feet.

"Okay, dude. Laters. I'll call you if anything happens."

"Yeah," Alex says forlornly, and turns away. Rickie watches him walk away and thinks about joining him. Instead, he turns back to the party.

CHAPTER 13

Rickie knows he *has* to recognize someone here. People continue to arrive. A large group pulls up in a limousine and gets out stretching and laughing and straightening their clothes. Rickie recognizes some of the boys as the drivers of lowered trucks and cars that they wheel into the school parking lot with sound systems pounding. The girls, to whom the boys now offer a hand with studied nonchalance, can usually be seen hanging on their arms or in a group laughing loudly and gossiping—*chismosas*. The boys stand at the curb calmly surveying the party on the other side of the fence and checking the street, while the girls continue to brush their dresses with their gloved hands or bend over to check lipstick and hair in the side mirrors of the limousine. They all glance Rickie's way when he moves away from the fence, but they do not give him a second look.

Rickie feels as inconsequential as they think he is. He's a loner, like a little boy, hanging onto a fence and on the outside looking

in. He is ready to leave and catch up with Alex when he recognizes the brown van that takes the place of the limousine at the curb.
It is what the car dealers call a California Conversion, a van cre-
ated specifically for people who wanted to replicate a living room
in a moving vehicle, and who didn't want to buy a lumbering RV.
The one time Claudia's father warmed up to Rickie was when the
man showed the boy the interior of the van, with its soft brown
seat cushions, the tall wrap-around seat backs, the brown rug on
the floor, and the little Venetian blinds at the teardrop side windows. Claudia's father scrubs and polishes it each weekend, but
there is no help for the faded and scaling exterior paint or for the
sun-bleached cushions and carpet, stained and matted by spilled
sweet drinks and greasy food. He babies this machine, always in-
specting it, ever vigilant for an unusual rattle or ping or knock,
and Rickie wonders why he cares so much; it's still going to fall
apart someday and end up dead in the driveway even if the man
drives it with maddening caution, rarely exceeding twenty miles
an hour on the local streets, or fifty on the freeways.

He pulls up carefully in back of the limousine as it is leaving
the curb.

"Rickie," Claudia calls as she pushes open the side door and
precedes her younger sisters out of the van. She runs up to him
and gives him a friendly but careful hug; she keeps a proper distance from him, knowing that the eyes of her parents are on her.

Claudia is dressed in a pale blue strapless gown and high
heels. Her black straight hair is pulled back from her forehead.
It shines in the light. She gained her woman's body when barely
fourteen, but her face retains some of the plump roundness of an
earlier self and some of the happy radiance. Her eyes are round
and dark. They used to have only a sweet teasing quality to them,

but now there's something new there, a hunger that Rickie knows the father recognizes and fears; the man doesn't like Rickie, even though the boy is always mumblingly respectful or simply quiet, standing at the door or in the living room looking down at his feet. He fears what Rickie has on his mind.

Rickie turns from Claudia and greets the mother quietly. The father pulls the van away from the curb to park it farther down the street, keeping the boy in sight in the passenger side mirror.

"*Como estas, mi'jo*? Are you going inside?" The mother, whose name is Merlinda, looks at him evenly, without judgment. He's just another awkward boy who cannot hold her gaze.

"I don't know."

"Aren't you going in?" Claudia asks.

"I wasn't invited. I was with Alex. We were just passing."

"You could go in with us. It's Gloria's sister's wedding party. You know, Gloria, from your English class. He can go in with us, can't he, '*Amá*?'"

"I don't think they want me here," he says.

Claudia and her mother both understand. "It is a party, *mi'jo*. Behave good and nothing goes wrong."

Rickie looks at Claudia's mother directly for the first time. She is wearing a shapeless black dress; he knows without thinking about it that it is her best dress, maybe her only dress-up dress. Her face, which had once been beautiful like Claudia's, has become heavy and lined, her eyes tired. But there is calm there, and it settles him.

"Nobody will care, Rickie. Anybody who might be trouble will be too drunk soon anyway," Claudia laughs.

"Come," the mother says. She gathers the little ones around her and looks for her husband. She sees him coming up the street.

"Let's go in now. I see *Papá* coming."

They approach the gate as the father joins them. He acknowledges Rickie with a nod and a grunt.

"Is he with you?" the security guard standing at the gate asks. Rickie recognizes him as a former star on the football team.

"Yes, he is with us," Claudia's mother answers. The guard looks over at his partner with a doubtful expression and then at Rickie.

"They don't want no trouble. This is their daughter's wedding." He looks hard at Rickie, but Rickie doesn't look back. The family shuffles through the gate past another group that has just arrived.

Once on the grounds they head for the light, looking for familiar faces, nodding at those sitting in the dimness of tables distant from the floodlights. Finally, Claudia's mother spots a family she recognizes. She takes Claudia by the arm and goes to them.

"*¡Hola! Buenas noches. Cómo están?*" she says. The husband and wife rise. Everyone shakes hands with quiet formality.

"*Muy bien. Y ustedes?*"

"*También. Disfrutando la fiesta?*"

"*Sí, sí.*"

The parents sit. Claudia holds out her hand for the couple's daughter who sits quietly in her elaborately ruffled pink dress.

"C'mon, *mi'ja*. Come with us. We'll go look around. Maybe we'll find some cute guys who will dance with us," she says.

The daughter catches her mother's eye, and she nods. The little girl jumps out of her chair. Claudia's sisters clap their hands excitedly.

Claudia takes the two younger girls' hands in each of hers. The group moves among the tables, Claudia and the girls in front,

Rickie in back. Rickie keeps his head down as they walk, only occasionally looking up, glancing at faces, sometimes finding questioning eyes focused on him, once a glimpse of a member of 18th Street leaning in and whispering in the ear of another and then turning and nodding in Rickie's direction. Rickie looks back down at his feet. He knows that if he stays, someone will come up to him before the night is over and challenge his right to be there. This isn't safe territory.

"Let's find Linda," Claudia says. She swings the arms of the two girls and heads for the house, looking for a knot of people. A photographer walks past them.

"Where's the bride?" Claudia asks him. He pauses, a big man with a kind, heavy face and wispy hair backlit by the floodlights from the house. "You're a cute one," he says. "Why don't I take your picture? You, too," he says to the little girls. "What are your names?"

The three little girls call their names, but the photographer doesn't pay attention.

"What's yours, sweetheart?" he asks of Claudia in a different tone of voice.

"Misty," Claudia says. Rickie looks at her and she laughs.

"Okay, Misty, get in the picture. C'mon, little ones. You, too," he says to Rickie. "Forgot your tux, huh?" he jokes, but Rickie doesn't reply or smile. "Okay, line up. Kinda like the cops, huh?" he jokes again. "Smile everybody." Claudia and the girls smile broadly. Claudia has a radiant, toothy smile framed by full and clearly sculpted lips. It is a smile that makes others think that she is always happy and sweet and not very bright. And she, herself, believes those things because no one tells her otherwise. Her world is *telenovelas* and the acquisition of inexpensive clothing and jewelry and make-up at the swap meet or from odd little stores buried in strip malls.

After the photographer has moved on, they continue toward the light in search of the bride.

"I don't feel right here," Rickie says. "I'm not dressed right."

"You look so fine. I could... Ohhh, I can't say," Claudia laughs.

"Let's go find some place," Rickie says, interested now and anxious to get away from there.

"What are we going to do with..?"

"Take them back."

"We want to find Linda," one of her sisters says.

"Okay, we'll go see Linda, and then I'll take you back."

They scan the area, looking over the dance floor, the front door to the house, the surrounding tables with candles flickering in the warm night air. Exhaust from cars still arriving, or from those passing slowly to check out what's going on, hangs in the air, which has only now begun to cool. Most people sit or stand with handkerchiefs in hand.

Finally, they find the bride, sprawled in a chair at one of the tables, exuding the magnanimity and ease of one who knows that this is her moment, laughing and talking with those gathered there, but also glancing about for her new husband who has disappeared. Rickie wouldn't trust him, and he sees that she doesn't fully trust him either.

"Linda, these little ones wanted to say hi," Claudia says. "Go, girls, give her a hug." Claudia gives them a gentle shove toward Linda.

"*Ven, mi'ja,*" Linda says, sitting up and holding out her arms for the smallest one. The little girl goes to her slowly, more interested in the beading on her lavish wedding dress than Linda herself.

Linda looks at Rickie and Claudia over the girls' heads. Rickie studies her face as she looks at Claudia. He knows these two don't like each other. Linda was forced to invite Claudia because their families know each other from church. She doesn't like Claudia because she's loud and draws attention to herself with her tight clothes. Linda must be glad her husband is not here right now; he'd be staring at Claudia's breasts, openly drinking in her body even on his wedding night.

Linda turns her attention to Rickie and stares directly into his eyes with a slight smile curling her lips. She takes in his thin, tightly-wound body; he stares back with the surety in his eyes that he could make her cry out in satisfaction, not like Carlos, that *Gordo*, who probably lies on top of her and huffs and puffs and falls off of her into a deep sleep before she is even close.

Rickie looks away before Claudia catches the look in his eyes.

"Thank you, sweethearts," Linda says, turning her attention back to the little girls. "I hope you have fun tonight. You guys, too," she says.

"You, too, you know, later," Claudia says and laughs loudly. The men at the table laugh with her. The young women shake their heads and look down.

"Me, too," one of the young men says.

"That's all you think about, you perv," his girlfriend answers and the others laugh.

Claudia and Rickie escort the girls back to the table where the two families sit. The men lean back in their chairs with their arms folded across their stomachs. They both look like they will begin dozing momentarily. The women sit next to each other, arms on the table, engaged in a lively conversation.

"Now where?" Rickie asks.

"Somewhere alone," Claudia answers and squeezes his hand. She moves closer to him and brushes against him. He looks at her as she does it again, and she laughs.

"Where?"

"Let's go around the side of the house. Maybe we'll find a place."

As they walk around the darkened side of the house, they come across a group smoking. It is too dark to see faces.

"Hey, baby, you want some?" one of them calls. Others in the group laugh.

"No, thanks. I've already got mine," she says and hugs Rickie's arm closer to her.

"Who the hell's that?"

Everyone in the group peers at Rickie in the darkness.

"He's that punk from Benton."

"Hey," Claudia says angrily, interrupting before anything more can be said. "This is a wedding and he isn't doing nothing to you. So smoke your *mota* and chill."

She marches Rickie past them into the backyard. His body has grown tense.

"They're going to come looking for us," he says.

"I know. Let's see if they got a back gate."

They step carefully across the backyard in the dark.

"I hope they don't have dogs," Claudia says. "These are new shoes." She laughs.

Rickie glances over his shoulder. No one is following them. They will, he knows. He squints his eyes to see in front of them. "I wish I had a flashlight," he says.

"I think I see a break in the fence.

They approach the fence carefully. The boards are dry and

splintery. Maybe kids or a heavy dog has pushed the fence apart. Or maybe on one of those nights when the winds howl out of the canyons and sweep across the valley floor, the old fence was rocked back and forth and was finally forced to give way. Claudia discovers that if she pushes one side and pulls the other, she can create a big enough gap to escape into the neighbor's backyard.

The boards creak as Rickie holds them apart for her.

"Watch your dress," he whispers. He gathers the material and tries to wrap it around her, but there is too much. A dog starts to bark inside the house in front of them. Floodlights on a motion sensor click on and cover the yard with light. They remain still, Claudia halfway through the fence.

"Should we go back?" she asks.

"No, wait. Let's see if anyone comes."

No one moves in the house, no shadow crosses in front of the light, no noise of footsteps.

"Go on," he whispers.

They clear the fence and walk quickly across the yard to the gate. The dog continues to bark, but no one quiets it. There is something hollow and forlorn and abandoned in the sound.

"Poor dog," Claudia says.

The gate along the side of the house is not locked. They open it carefully and walk into the front yard. Light from the street shows a yard rank and wild with weeds and untended Saint Augustine grass stretching a network of runners onto the walkway, nearly covering it. Someone has laid a square of sod near the sidewalk, but it has browned and dried.

"I think that fool, what's his name, the *mayate*, Herbie, that's the one, he lives here."

"I don't know him," Claudia says.

"Yeah, you do. He sells. He must be out on the job tonight. Look at this place. For all the money he makes, you'd think..." Rickie doesn't finish his statement. A car approaches slowly. They move closer to the wall that parallels the driveway and watch the car go by. An older couple, no threat. Rickie goes out to the curb and looks up and down the block.

"C'mon. It's not that far. " He takes her hand and begins to trot down and around the block.

"What?" she asks, gathering up her dress with her free hand as she follows.

"An empty house. I was there today getting high with Alex."

"Do you have any with you?"

"No, Alex had it."

"Don't run too fast. These shoes..."

Rickie looks over his shoulder at the empty street and slows down. When they get to the house, he leads her past the broken glass on the driveway and in through the rear door. The pale blue light from the street stretches across the floor of the living room and softens the bleak emptiness of the room.

They sit where he and Alex sat that afternoon, backs against the wall. She kicks her shoes off.

"My feet hurt," she says.

"Here. I'll rub them for you."

She looks at him for a moment with mild disbelief because he so rarely offers anything, and then she crosses her right leg over her left so he can rub that foot.

"Feel my leg," she says. "It's smooth. I shaved."

He runs his hand along her ankle and her calf. She rubs his back.

"Why don't you take your shirt off? I want to feel your back."

Rickie unbuttons the top buttons of his shirt and pulls it over his head. There is no fat on his body; baseball has kept him lean.

She begins to rub his back, but absently. He turns to look at her. She gives him a sad, fleeting smile; tears have filled her eyes.

"What's wrong?" he asks.

"Nothing," she says, rubbing his back again, quicker now, as though wanting to get it done. "I was thinking how much I love to rub my little sisters' backs, and their pudgy feet. They have the softest skin."

They sit without speaking for a minute.

"Do you love me, Rickie?" she asks, and he hears the resignation in her voice. She knows to expect the same perfunctory answer she hears her aunts and her cousins get from their husbands and boyfriends, and they seem to laugh it off. She will, too, Rickie knows.

"Yeah, of course I do." He keeps his back to her.

"Would you rub my back?"

"You'll have to undo your dress. I can only get your shoulders."

"You unzip it."

She turns so that her back is to him. He unzips her dress. She slips it off her shoulders and onto her lap. The tops of her breasts are pale and smooth in the dim light. He reaches around and cups them with his hands.

"Not yet, Rickie," she says. "Rub my back. You said."

He withdraws his hands and places them on her shoulders, massaging lightly with his thumbs.

"That feels good. I wish we had something to smoke," she says. "Or drink. I'm too ... nervous."

"You don't have to be. We've been together a long time," he says, gently massaging her neck.

"Don't mess up my hair. I'll never put it right again. My mom will know something's gone on if my hair is messy. She thinks you're dangerous because you're so quiet." She giggles.

"I'm not dangerous," he says and bites her neck. "I'm just a vampire."

"No hickies," she says pulling her shoulder away. "I'll get killed."

"Then let me bite your lips."

She turns sideways, and he takes her bottom lip with his lips.

"Kiss me, Rickie," she says and opens her mouth for his tongue. She turns against him and places his hand on her breast.

"Do I feel good to you?" she asks at last.

"What do you think? You're driving me crazy. I want you."

"Do you have anything?"

"No, of course not. I didn't think anything was going to happen. I was on my way home, remember?" He wants to feel blameless.

"Oh, I thought boys always had something in their wallets," she says. "I'm sorry."

They don't speak for a moment; he does not touch her.

"If we do it, you know, don't let yourself come inside me, okay? Maybe we'll be okay," she relents. She rises to ease off her dress. She stands before him self-consciously in the pale light wearing only her bra and panties, her body fully a woman's. He stares at her.

"Don't," she laughs nervously. "What about you? Are you just going to sit there and stare?"

He take off his shoes and socks and stands, undoes his belt and lets his pants fall. He stands before her fully erect.

"Oh, my God," she says softly. "Come here."

Everything happens quickly and awkwardly. Both of them know the place is wrong. Other people have the backseat of a car at least, or someone's bedroom when parents are away. Not this, not the hard floor of an abandoned house.

He wishes they had gone slowly, kissing and touching and enjoying one another's bodies the way he has seen lovemaking in movies. But they hadn't. Too soon they are lying on the floor on her clothes spread out beneath them. Then it's over. He doesn't remove himself.

Almost immediately they are up and dressing. They don't speak. Claudia goes carefully to the bathroom where she finds toilet tissue still in a holder on the wall. When she comes back, she inspects the dress for stains, holding it away from her and checking the material carefully.

"I might get pregnant, you know. You were supposed to come out." She tries to keep the disappointment and the anger and the sadness out of her voice, but she can't. It doesn't matter. He doesn't really hear her. He has his own disappointment: what has been built up as some great experience has proved to be not much different from masturbation—the pleasure too momentary and leaving a reverberating hollowness when it's over, like a walk down a long and dark and empty corridor.

"It happened too fast," he says.

"Would you like to be a daddy?" she asks, hoping to salvage some tenderness from this moment.

"I don't know. Maybe," he adds. He knows that's the answer she wants. A kid won't be his responsibility. She and her mom will take care of it. That's the way it is with all of his friends.

"I wonder if you'll be a good one," she says.

"It hasn't happened," he says curtly. He ties his Nikes, adjusts the laces neatly and stands. "C'mon, we gotta get back before they send people after us."

They walk back to the party. They do not speak except when she asks him to take her hand.

"Remember, I'm a little shaky in these heels," she says, looking for comfort. He says nothing, but he does take her hand. The night is cooling rapidly. She walks close to him. They follow the loud music back to the party.

When they get to the gate, she asks him if he's hungry or wants to dance.

"No, I'm going to go."

"Where?"

"I don't know. Home, I guess. Maybe Alex's."

"Stay with me."

He looks at her blankly, slightly disgusted by her too wide smile, her lips that are too full, and her full body. She has been just as he thought she would be—too easy. He will come back when he wants her, but he will never love her. As soon as he thinks this, he feels the beginnings of tenderness towards her.

"No," he says softly. "Your parents hate me. They don't want to see you with me. I gotta go."

He turns and walks away with his hands in his pockets. He doesn't look back to see the desolate look on her face.

"That punk's a fool," one of the security guards says to Claudia. "He doesn't know how to treat a fine girl like yourself."

"I'm still here, baby," his partner at the gate says. "I'm a hell of a lot better than him. You should try me out."

"Sure thing," Claudia says. She manages a smile and looks more closely at the two of them. Both are tall with close cropped hair and little goatees. They are in their mid twenties. Their bodies are lean and muscular from lifting weights.

"Maybe I'll bring you guys something to eat later on. Are you hungry?"

"Only for you," the first one says.

She laughs and walks by them.

"You're so full of shit," his partner says when she's out of earshot.

"Maybe, but I bet I get laid tonight. Man, she is *fine*."

Rickie sprints home, as much to escape the sense of deflation and failure that wraps around him and weighs him down as to get out of the unfriendly neighborhood. He wishes now that he had gone straight home with Alex.

SUNDAY MORNING

CHAPTER 14

Berta rises at her usual hour. Sunday. Church day. Today she thinks she might leave a little later so that she can sit alone in the back. It would be insulting to Father Bernal to arrive early and sit there. He would find a way to say something. "Why do you sit so far away, Berta? Do you feel like communing with God on your own today?" he would say and laugh, but she would feel a gentle criticism behind the laugh and the soft words.

Today she will arrive just as the doors are closing. She does not want to sit up front in the crush of ladies with their fans and squirming children and the young boys and girls making eyes at one another. She wants to be by herself. Is that wrong? Will Father tell her it is vanity to want to sit alone and enjoy the dimness at the back of the church and the quiet and the cool air that smells like candles and incense and prayer books, and the breath of a thousand prayers and mournful sighs that smell like Father's breath when he speaks so close to you? He is a soft man who feels sorry for himself, perhaps because he doubts his faith and calling but cannot find the courage to act. She can see it in his face, in his soft cheeks that sag into jowls, the black stubble of his beard against the pastiness of his skin, in his eyes that bully you with a perpetual squint behind his thick wire-frame glasses.

Berta wants to be apart from everyone else today, she doesn't know why. She wants to let her eyes roam from one sunlit window to the next without feeling Father's eyes squinting in accusation at her.

So she will arrive late and sit in the back and allow the dim coolness to envelop her and carry her through the kneeling and standing, praying and responding, her Rosary familiar and comfortable in her hands, in a kind of dream state that will take her drifting on the drone of Father's words and the music and prayer, oblivious to everything in particular except for the sound of Father's voice and the responses of the congregation, and cool air and the smooth wood of the back of the pew in front of her, polished by the hands of hundreds of supplicants on the way to or from their knees. And if Father Bernal asks, she will say she rose late, that's all.

Berta busies herself in the kitchen, making herself a small pot of coffee. There will be enough for another cup after service today. In a few minutes she will brush her hair and wash her face and put on her church dress. She will walk to church slowly.

She looks about the kitchen with its old wooden cabinets painted yellow by Osvaldo years ago, and she does not find anything to straighten or put away. Everything is in order, and she is satisfied. She will sit down when her coffee is ready and relax for a minute or two. She does not even want to hear the TV. She goes to the back door to check the morning.

As she opens the door, a man wearing a worn black sports jacket who has been sitting on the top step with his back against the screen door springs up, banging the screen door as he does so. Berta lets out a startled cry and draws back. The man stumbles off the steps on to the hardened dirt of the backyard.

"¡*Ay, Madre de Dios*! You scared me, 'Amá. I must've fallen asleep in the sun," he says as he peels off the jacket. "Too hot."

"Ricardo? What are you doing here?" Berta asks.

"Can't I visit my own mother?" he asks. He shades his eyes with one hand as he looks at her standing in the doorway. She is surprised to see that his hair is still black and his face unlined. His eyes are large and moist.

"You don't seem happy to see me," he says peevishly.

"I know that men who go away unannounced and return unannounced do not go and return from love," she says, not moving from behind the door.

"I'll go away again," he says, but they both know he does not mean it.

She opens the door and scans the backyard as though checking for someone else.

"No one else, 'Amá. Just me."

She moves aside to let him enter, and then she sits down at her place at the table. He stands in the center of the kitchen and looks around.

"Still the same."

"Why should it change? Who would do the work?" she asks, threads of disappointment and accusation in her words.

Ricardo does not respond. "What time is Mass?" he asks finally.

"Now. And at eleven."

"I'm hungry. I'll take you to breakfast. Can you go to the eleven?"

She is going to protest, to tell him it will be hotter later, the cool air will be gone, but she does not. She knows her son has returned to ask for something, and she is curious to know what it is.

They drive without speaking to the same restaurant where Daisy and Rickie went the day before. The radio in the car is tuned to the American music station. When Ricardo sees her frown at it, he snaps it off.

One time she had gone through Rickie's notebook as it lay on his bed. She found what looked like a poem in Rickie's own handwriting. She struggled through the first few lines and was disgusted by what she thought she read there. When she asked him about it later, he told her it was a song.

"A song? With words like that?" she asked. She was sitting in her usual chair at the kitchen table.

"That's how songs are these days." He stood at the refrigerator with the door open.

"Did you write it? Close the door. You will let all the cold out."

"No, I didn't write it."

"It is not right. It is disgusting and tells lies."

"It's just a song," Rickie said. "It doesn't mean anything." He closed the refrigerator door and leaned against it.

"I don't want you to think about women with those words. You should be respectful. Those people hate women."

"You shouldn't go through my stuff," Rickie said.

"You are my grandchild. You live in my house."

"But still..."

Though she reserved the right to do it, she did not go through his backpack or his dresser drawers again; she did not want to know more than she could truly comprehend. He was more careful where he left his notebook and papers as well.

Berta sits across from her son at the little table. She remains unspeaking, hands folded in front of her and eyes cast down, with a stillness that is like prayer. She waits to discover why he has finally come to see her. She and Osvaldo sacrificed much to give him a chance in America, but she knows he has not been able to accept life's hardships as she and his father had, nor has he been strong enough to make the sacrifices they made. She blames herself.

He stands quickly when he is called to pick up their food, clearly relieved that the spell of silence is broken. After he returns and places the empty tray on the next table, he sits down and eats hungrily. She watches him without comment.

He pushes his plate away and wipes his mouth with a bunch of napkins he tears absently from the dispenser. She picks through her burrito and removes fatty pieces of pork, placing them at the side of her plate.

"So, 'Amá," he says, "how have you been?"

"Things have changed and I have gotten by," she replies. She does not look up from her food.

He waits, but nothing more is forthcoming. "That's it? Nothing more?"

"What would you have me say?" She looks at him now. "Your father died and there was no one but these children and a few neighbors. You, his only son, were not there."

"I didn't know," he complains. "Do you think I chose not to be there? I loved my father."

"You made your choice. You left in a shameful way, my son.

You gave in to what is lowest in you."

"I don't want to hear about it."

"You will listen, if only for one last time." She stares into his eyes until he can hold her gaze no longer. He has become a stranger.

"Your father was a man of great heart and pride. No man could say of him that he did not take responsibility for his family. No man could say that he was lazy. No man could say of him that he permitted circumstance to make him less--"

"And I am not my father. Is that what you are trying to say? I know that! But what is his greatness doing for him now? He's dead, worked to death in a country that was not his, that had no use for him except to use him up."

"But he was a man!" she says forcefully. A few people at the order counter turn around to look. She looks down at her hands in apology. "You must be a man as well," she says quietly.

"I *am* a man. This is useless. We're getting nowhere. I came down to see you --"

"Why now? Why not before? Why not when I needed you?"

He sighs resignedly. "Life is more…complex. Your life, *Papá's* life, were different. You brought rules here from a simpler time and place." He pauses. "I… couldn't come home before. I admit it, '*Amá*, I did some things I'm not proud of. Not just the girl. Other things, too. But I have tried to make them right, things you don't know about. I want to make things right with you and my children."

"Why now?" she says without softness.

"Daisy has written me letters. She is worried about Junior. I want to take him back with me."

Berta waves a hand as though brushing a fly away. She sits back in her chair.

"So now you are ready to be a father. As you wish. He is your son. I cannot keep him if he wants to go. Make sure, my son, that this is not just another of your crazy ideas like the fourteen-year-old, which you learn to regret later on."

He looks as though he is about to snap back at her for mentioning the girl, but doesn't. He looks out the window.

"Look at this place, 'Amá."

She looks around the little restaurant. "What am I supposed to see?"

"Not just the restaurant. The whole place, outside. Trash, dirt, the walls are written on, windows broken, the apartment buildings are dangerous, the streets are dangerous. Gangs all over the place. Nobody cares or does anything about it. Look, just look."

Just then, two teenaged boys walk by. Each wears a T-shirt a size too big and jeans belted low on the rear end. Their heads are shaven, and they wear sunglasses on the back of their heads. Folded blue bandanas hang from back pockets. They walk slowly, stiffly, eyes glancing at their feet, to the street, ahead, at their reflection in the window, and down and to the side, in a constant play of self-consciousness, arrogance and wariness. They see the man and the old lady looking at them from the restaurant window as they pass, and they stare back for a dangerous moment. Ricardo shifts his eyes away to watch a young woman in the crosswalk who is looking over her shoulder and extending her hand and telling a little boy to hurry. Berta does not look away. A passing car honks and the boys turn quickly.

"Whether you want to admit it or not, these are Junior's friends. Maybe not these gangsters particularly, but ones just like them. Daisy says he's already been in trouble. He'll keep on getting into trouble until he goes to jail or worse. He needs to get out of here. Up there the schools are better. I'll be able to watch after him. He needs a man in his life, someone to guide him."

"And you are that man," she says without bitterness.

"I have become one."

"Why now? Why do you want him now? School is not out yet. It is almost summer."

"That's the reason. It's almost summer." He stops; he has finally heard what she has said. "His school isn't out yet?"

"No. Another two weeks."

"Oh, I thought he might be finished. Friday was the last day for schools in Ventura." His disappointment is obvious, but then he brightens. "Okay, two weeks then. I'll come back. My apartment is near the beach. He might be able to get a job where I work--"

"Where do you work?"

"I am the assistant manager at a store in Ventura. Klein's. Have you heard of it?"

Berta shakes her head. "What is it?"

"A place that sells affordable furniture."

"Is the job good?"

"It pays good. Good benefits."

Berta sits back in her chair. She is willing to wait and see.

When he says he wants to see Billy in Pacoima, Berta's only comment is that Billy is still very angry with him, even after all of these years.

"I just want to see where he lives," is Ricardo's only comment.

They drive on surface streets past the junkyards and the huge holes in the earth from which crushed rock and gypsum and lime were once extracted, and which later have become landfills or simply remain deep and empty craters fenced off to the public; past the *panderias* and *carnecercias* and the little hole-in-the-wall restaurants advertising *mariscos*, and the hundreds of anonymous little store fronts that come and go. They drive toward Sylmar, one town bleeding into the next with no noticeable change. The day is warming and becoming smoggy. Shapes become indistinct, too bright in sunlight whitened by the haze. Ricardo squints behind sunglasses from the glare, from the acid hanging in the air.

They drive without speaking until they reach Bill's neighborhood. Berta gives Ricardo directions onto his street.

Bill lives in an apartment building behind a tall, black wrought iron fence. On the other side of the fence, a small strip of tired grass runs up to the beige stucco. A big area of the lower portion of the street-facing facade has been painted a greyer shade of beige, but ghosts of black graffiti are still visible beneath the paint.

The gate is locked. Ricardo rattles it and looks hopefully at the windows facing the street. There is movement behind one of them.

"Billy," Ricardo calls. "Bill."

He stands there for some minutes, shakes the gate again, but no one looks out a window or comes out of a doorway. Ricardo turns back toward the car.

"I'll try calling him," he says after he gets in.

Berta says nothing. She watches him turn the fan on high and sit back to let the cold air blow on his face and throat and chest as he dials the number. In a moment he says: "Voicemail. I got his voicemail. I left him a message last night that I would probably be here only today. Do you think he'll call?"

Berta looks up at the windows of the apartment building.

"Maybe. It would be better for you to talk with him face to face."

When they return to Berta's house, Rickie is standing at the open front door with his arms folded. He watches the man get out of the car and stand with the door open, looking over the roof of the car at him.

"*Hola, mi'jo,*" Ricardo says.

Rickie tries to process this stranger before him. Clean-shaven, in his early forties, his face round and mournful, hair cut short and neat. He wears a pale blue wash-and-wear short sleeve shirt and black pants. Rickie waits for the man to speak.

"I come to see you play," Ricardo says finally. "Are you playing today?"

"It's Sunday. We don't play Sunday." Rickie is disdainful. Suddenly, he remembers why he should have gotten up earlier—Coach Vega talked yesterday about a light practice, hitting and catching some flies. He was going to buy doughnuts for the ones who showed up. With jealousy directed at the ones who did turn out and regret at the missed opportunity to hang out with Coach and listen to his baseball stories and his philosophies about growing up and the neighborhood and being Latino, Rickie feels even greater anger at this man who he realizes is his father and has shown up out of the blue.

"Why're you here? Are you in trouble? Running from the cops?"

"You don't need to know my story. Don't worry about it," Ricardo says. The tone is supposed to be tough and indifferent, but it sounds childish, as though he's taking part in some school-yard argument.

"I wanted to see my family," he says in a conciliatory manner. "I've made some mistakes, *mi'jo*. I wanted to see what I could do to change things."

"Are you going to stay down here?"

"No, I'm going back up."

Rickie relaxes a little at this news.

"I want you to go with me," Ricardo adds.

"You want me to go with you? I don't even know you. You don't know me." He looks to his grandmother for support, for an acknowledgement of the outrageousness of this idea, but she sits in the car and stares straight ahead.

"What do you need to know? I'm your father." Anger has crept back into his voice. "It's better up there," he begins again. "Cleaner. Nicer."

Rickie struggles to understand the significance of his father's words. "What would I do up there?"

"Go to school. Play baseball. I don't know, the same things you do here."

"What about my friends?"

"What about them? You'll make new ones up there."

"What about your fourteen-year-old girlfriend? Don't you have any babies with her?" The anger rises up in Rickie's throat like choking bile. "You'll run off again when you can't take it no more."

They are too distant, too loud, speaking to one another from the street to the house.

"I was a lot younger then, *mi'jo*," Ricardo says softly, approaching his son. "Things are different now. Yolanda went back to her family years ago. I don't have any babies to take care of. I got a good job and a nice apartment near the beach. Things are good up there. You'd like it. And it would take you away from this."

"What's wrong with this? This is my 'hood. I don't want to leave it." As though to make his point, like it is the established rhythm and melody of the neighborhood, a plane takes off and roars loudly overhead. Ricardo says nothing for a moment.

"What do you want?" Rickie asks when the sound has diminished. "Show up out of nowhere, some stranger I don't even know, and expect me to jump around like a little kid and say, 'Daddy, daddy!' No way, dude. You're a ghost to me. I don't know you. I'm not going," Rickie says.

"We'll see."

"I'm not *going*." Rickie turns and goes inside. When Ricardo follows him inside a few seconds later, he finds Rickie standing by the sofa on his cell phone.

"I'll meet you there in a few minutes," he says. He looks defiantly at his father.

"I'm coming back after school is out. We'll talk about it then and decide," Ricardo says, but doubt plays across his face.

"I've already made my decision. I'm not going. Go back up to Ventura and your lonely apartment and your job."

Rickie walks past him back out the front door. Ricardo grabs his arm.

"Don't!" Rickie yells, turning to face Ricardo and stare with deadly fearlessness into the man's eyes. "Don't put your fucking hands on me!"

Berta reads the look in the boy's eyes and watches his hands tighten into fists; Ricardo lets him go. Father and son are strangers to one another. Ricardo doesn't know him; Junior doesn't consider himself the man's son. Berta watches as a new revelation takes over her son's features, a revelation so saddening and profound that it roots the man where he stands at the front door: he really doesn't *want* to know this boy. The boy is too distant, too unknown, and what he does see in his son he doesn't like.

And Ricardo doesn't have a home here any longer. He walked out on them years ago and his family is gone from him. He isn't this boy's father in any meaningful way and never will be. His older son wants nothing to do with him. His younger son is unknown to him, a surly boy with a shaved head and a cold face. Maybe his daughter cares about him, maybe Daisy...or is she just curious? Berta knows about the letters and phone calls between father and daughter. Will Daisy eventually close off to him, too, when she realizes he is not the person she has envisioned? Will the letters stop? Will they become cards with empty words on them and then nothing at all?

Berta looks down at her hands in despair. She has no answers for them. From the time of Osvaldo's death, she has wanted to be able to depend on Ricardo and her grandchildren to help her navigate life in the United States and in Los Angeles, but Ricardo was gone until now and her grandchildren barely hold on with jobs and school and haven't the time for anything else.

Ricardo turns as Junior crosses the little front yard, opens the gate and lets it slam behind him. He watches his son march angrily away, and then he looks around the neighborhood. Berta looks, too. Sunday. Quiet. The sky white and diffuse. Another stifling hot day.

"What will you do?" Berta asks.

"I will see Daisy and then go back up there; I can't stand this heat."

Ricardo looks down at what he is wearing. "I should have worn something different, better," he says to no one as he smooths his shirt. "She would have liked that, like one of the handsome men in the *novelas*." He looks at his mother to see if she understands. She does. She remembers going to Santa Monica one time when Osvaldo was still alive, years ago. They had driven the old pick-up to the beach to escape heat like today. While Osvaldo talked and joked with the men fishing off the pier, she watched the lost men who walked the pier that Sunday afternoon and looked longingly at the parading families and the couples eating outside at little tables and holding hands and laughing. Her son reminds her of those men—rootless and unloved. Her heart aches for him: he had wanted Junior to save him from himself. What had he been thinking!

CHAPTER 15

They are sitting on the bleachers—Alex, Dennis and Oscar—when Rickie gets there. Rickie sees the coach's pick-up leaving the parking lot. Players crowd together in the box and in the front seat.

"Your coach was just here," Alex says. "He asked about you, if you were coming. I told him I didn't know."

Regretfully, Rickie watches the pick-up turn and disappear.

"I should have been here earlier. He's taking them to go get doughnuts."

"You didn't go to church either?" Dennis asks. "Tony must a been the only one."

When Rickie doesn't respond, Alex says, "I didn't want to go. Too freakin' hot. My mom took my little sisters."

"Why they want to go there anyway?" Oscar says. "All's they hear is the same stuff every week, about how God loves them and shit. If God loves them so much, how come we live here?"

"Did you go to early Mass?" Dennis asks Rickie.

"Stupid. I don't go to church. My grandma does, I don't." He looks at Dennis with disgust.

"Soor-ree," Dennis says in ironic apology. "What's up your butt?"

"*¿Que onda contigo?*" Alex asks Rickie as he stares at Dennis to shut him up.

"Nothing. I had a fight with my old man."

"Your dad? I thought he was long gone," Oscar says. Everyone has heard about him running away with the fourteen-year-old years ago.

"He was. He showed up this morning. I don't know why."

"He start bossing you around, telling you shit?" Dennis asks.

"No." Rickie looks at Alex. "He wants me to go up to Ventura or Oxnard or some place up there."

"Damn, dude, they've got some fine girls up there. This one time I went up there for the Strawberry Festival..." Dennis begins.

"When does he want you to go?" Alex interrupts.

"Right after school is out. I told him no."

"Is he an asshole like my old man?" Oscar asks.

"I don't know. No. Maybe. I don't know what he's like. It's not that."

"Dude, it's gotta be better than this," Alex says. "We're dying here. It's either too freakin' hot or raining and flooded. It doesn't matter. Look at it. It always looks dead. Just dirt and sand and dust and weeds. Even the trees look like they're dying."

A scattering of five little clouds hangs over the mountains to the east. The heat pulls on them and draws them down to earth like white goatees. Curiously out of place in an otherwise cloudless sky, they seem full of portent.

"Shit, dude," Dennis says anxiously. "Something's going to happen today. Like an earthquake or some shit."

No one responds. The sun beats down on the dirt field and the dry grey wood of the bleachers smoothed by the jeans and skirts of parents, brothers and sisters who have rooted for some boy or girl long departed from childhood.

All at once, they get up and move to the shade of a thick syca-more tree whose lower leaves are coated with dust; without rain or watering, they're already turning brown. Dennis stands at the trunk of the tree looking for bark to peel.

"Didn't Indians used to write on the bark of these trees?" he asks.

"Stupid, dude, that was the Indians some place else. They wrote on birch bark," Oscar says.

"They could've wrote on this stuff," Dennis says.

"It *is* nice up there, dude," Alex says quietly to Rickie. "You ever been?" They sit cross-legged together in the shade.

"No."

"My mom took me up there to Ventura. They've got this har-bor with all these shops around it and restaurants and sailboats..."

"That's not where my old man lives, you can count on it. He probably lives in the part of town just like this. Apartments and garbage all over the place and homies just like us."

"I don't think there is a part of town like this up there. I didn't see it. It looked nice to me. I wouldn't mind living there."

"Maybe you should go live with my old man," Rickie says, the anger rising in his voice. The other two are quiet. Alex is a nice guy. Nobody ever gets mad at him, not even Rickie. Alex doesn't say anything. He stares at the dirt in front of him as though it holds some important message.

"Hey, let's go to the park, man, and swim," Oscar calls to them. He has joined Dennis at the sycamore tree, which he is gouging with his knife, laying open the flesh of the tree.

"Can't. No water," Rickie says.

"Yeah, there is. I was just there."

"Asshole, there isn't," Rickie says. He stares hard at Oscar.

"Why're you calling me asshole, *ese*?" Oscar asks, stepping out from behind the tree.

"You think you know fucking everything just because you come from Pacoima."

Oscar leaves the tree and comes to stand over Rickie.

"What do you know, fucker?"

There is a flat, emotionless look in Rickie's eyes as he stares at the brittle grass in front of him.

"Back off, *pendejo*," Alex says, pushing hard on Oscar's knee with his open hand. Oscar gives way and falls back a few steps.

"Hey, dude, that's my sore knee."

"Then back off and shut up," Alex says. "Some fool tagged the building and threw a whole bunch of dog shit and other stuff into the pool. It ruined the filter. They had to close it down to drain it. I heard it won't open 'til the 4th of July. So go back to your tree."

"Dumb shit," Oscar says and turns back to the tree and stabs it with his knife.

"Let's get out of here," Alex says to Rickie. "I'm hungry. Are you?"

"I don't care," he says, but he gets up when Alex gets up.

"Hey, where're you guys going?" Dennis asks.

"Get something to eat."

Though uninvited, Dennis and Oscar follow.

"Let's go to Johnnie's," Dennis says. Nobody responds, but

they're headed that way, in the direction of Landerman.

People are out now, washing cars, watering lawns, coming home from church, from the store, from Sunday morning breakfast at *El Mexicano* or one of the other small take-out restaurants. Everyone eyes the four boys in the low-belted pants and T-shirts and close-cropped hair; everyone keeps track of them out of the corners of their eyes because they are a pack and dangerous. One or two might not be a problem, but they're always a problem in a group. People who approach them on the sidewalk glance down to check the boys' hands to see if they hold anything and then look up quickly at the eyes to decode any sign of trouble there.

They come out on to Landerman and head south on the wide boulevard. A cop car pulls up and drives at a crawl to stay parallel with them and check them out. After shadowing them for a hundred feet, the car speeds off with the siren on.

Alex and Rickie walk without speaking. Oscar and Dennis walk behind and respond to the attention being paid them by talking and laughing loudly, calling to girls in cars, elbowing each other, and commenting on people they pass on the street.

"Hey, wait a minute," Oscar says. He and Dennis have stopped and are looking at a display window. Alex and Rickie walk back to them.

"'Tom's Stereo,'" Dennis reads. "I never seen this place."

"It's been here for years, *menso*," Alex said. "The guy fixes old stereos. Maybe he sells new ones, I don't know."

"No way."

"Yes, *buey*."

"We could be in and out in a minute," Oscar says.

"You want to go inside?" Dennis doesn't get it.

"I'll bet the place isn't even alarmed," Oscar says. He's lost in thought.

When they open the door, it trips a little bell. It is dark and cool inside. Oscar takes off his sunglasses.

"Old school," he whispers to Dennis. "Easy, dogg."

Boxes of stereo components and flat screen TVs are stacked in the middle of the floor. Smaller items like MP3 players, phones, and digital cameras are in locked display cases. A DJ's turntable sits on the counter. In back of the counter, a broad man with fat, indelicate fingers is chewing his lunch and wiping his mouth. He has emerged from a little partitioned-off room behind a curtain. A glance through the partially open curtain reveals the contents of a bag lunch spread on a worktable next to bits and pieces of a receiver.

He looks the boys over carefully. His face is tired, his eyes wary.

"Got anything cheap?" Dennis asks.

"Got any money?" the man asks in return, sure that the boy does not.

"Can't we take a look?" Alex asks.

"For a minute." He keeps a close eye on the boys as they move around the store. The boys spread out.

"Can I see this MP3 player?" Rickie asks.

"Just look at it in the case."

"I can't even see it?" Rickie asks. The others look up as well.

"Bring some money next time and I'll let you see it."

"How do you know I ain't got money?"

"Okay, show it to me. If you got enough, I'll hold on to it and you can look at the player."

"What?" Rickie asks, incredulously.

"Collateral," the man says. "Do you know what that means?"

Rickie does know what the word means; he learned it from teachers who ask for something in return for the pencils or pens he borrows in class.

"Man, this store is whacked. No wonder you don't do any business."

"I think it's time for you boys to leave."

"You don't like Mexicans, do you?" Oscar says. They have all come up to the counter.

"You don't know what you're talking about," the man says wearily. "Just leave."

"Maybe we don't feel like leaving. We ain't doin' nothing," Oscar says.

Rickie sees the man glance below the counter; he has something hidden there, a bat or a gun. Alex sees it, too. "Okay," Alex says. "Let's go. There's nothin' here we want anyway."

"Who you going to sell to if it ain't us?" Dennis asks.

"I don't know, kid. Maybe nobody. Maybe I'll close the place. Then you all can go to Best Buy."

"You can go to hell," Oscar says as he walks toward the door.

"This ain't no Best Buy," Rickie says.

They file out of the store. Dennis closes the door hard so that the glass shudders and the little bell jangles crazily. When they get out on the sidewalk, Rickie turns and surveys the place without speaking.

"What're you thinking, Rickie?" Alex asks.

"That fool doesn't belong in this neighborhood. He's a racist. You hear him talk about Mexicans?"

"He didn't say nothing. Oscar did."

Rickie stares at him for a long moment. Finally he says, "He didn't have to say nothing. You could feel it in that place."

"We oughta hit this place, dogg. Clean it out. That'll get him out of the 'hood," Oscar says. "We could do it tonight. I say we do it," he says and looks at the others. Dennis looks to Rickie expectantly, but Rickie and Alex act like they don't hear Oscar.

"It would be easy, dude," Dennis says. "We could be in and out before the cops ever get here. Just grab some stuff and go. I could bring my little brother's wagon, dude. We could load it up with a badass system." He mugs scratching like a DJ and makes bass and drum noises with his mouth.

"What's the matter with you two?" Oscar asks of Rickie and Alex, who walk in front of him. "You scared? This crew is fucked."

Rickie stops walking and turns around. Everyone else stops as well. Rickie stares at Oscar, who grows tense as he waits for Rickie to do something.

"What the fuck is with you, dude?" Rickie says. Out the corner of his eye, he can see that pedestrians on the opposite side of the street have stopped to watch. On their side, people gather in front and in back of them.

"More cops," Alex says. "Coming down Landerman. Start walking."

The four boys begin to move again. People on both sides of the street join them, but they eye the four nervously, worried that something might still develop; they are anxious to get where they're going. The cop on the passenger side eyes the boys as the car passes slowly by, but he doesn't say anything. The car continues on.

"I'm hungry," Alex says finally to break the silence.

"I don't got any money," Dennis says.

"I got enough for me only," Oscar says.

"How about you?" Rickie asks Alex.

"I got a couple of dollars. Not enough for all of us."

Rickie looks at the other two, wishing they'd disappear. They stand and wait.

"My old man gave me some," Rickie says finally.

"I thought you and him fought," Alex says.

"We did. He didn't actually give it to me. I found his wallet on the sofa. He had more than a hundred bucks in there, so I grabbed some. He can afford it," he says by way of defense, but no one is accusing him. It wasn't his father's wallet; it was his grandmother's, but he doesn't say it. He rarely takes money from her, adhering to a code of honor that holds that, no matter how much he wants or needs money, he doesn't take it from her unless he asks. If she says no, he accepts it. But this time, his anger at her for just sitting there and saying nothing got the best of him. Her worn men's wallet sat on the arm of the sofa; she had been paid yesterday by the lady in Burbank, and the wallet was fat, at least to his eyes. He will tell her later if she doesn't already know by the time he gets home.

The four boys continue down Landerman until they reach the restaurant. They escape the late morning heat in the shade of the overhang and scan the menu above the order window—hamburgers, burritos, tacos, and *menudo* on the weekends. The swamp cooler is already on inside, forcing the strong smell of *menudo* out the order window. Rickie doesn't eat it. It reminds him of the locker room smell at school and the *mensos* who get so drunk on Friday and Saturday nights that they don't notice the bits of food and saliva mingled with the greasy sweat on their stupid faces; men who spit when they accost you on the street, coming toward you in their marionette stagger and stumble, hand out for money to buy *menudo* to help them sober up before trying to find Sunday work on street corners. Not him.

Rickie pays for Alex and Dennis; his generosity lessens the guilt at stealing the money. They sit at one of the concrete tables alongside the restaurant. The tables have been tagged and scoured, tagged and scoured again, over and over, the ghosts of names creating a crazed pattern on the table tops. Others have scribed their names on the once polished surfaces or simply gouged holes in the benches or the tabletops on long and boring afternoons. The boys eat without speaking and read the graffiti to find evidence of themselves or of people they know. The sounds of passing traffic and people ordering and food being prepared inside the little restaurant provide the rhythm against which they push the food into their mouths. When they finish, they shove all the trash to the edge of the table and sit back. Oscar lights a cigarette. Rickie and Alex sit with elbows on the table, holding their chins in their hands. Dennis finds a bottle cap and scribes his tag in the stone. The rest of the day yawns emptily before them. No pool to swim in and too hot to do anything else.

"Dude, it's quiet on Sundays," Dennis says, not looking up from his work.

"What are those real noisy planes?" Oscar asks.

"Private jets."

"Man, sometimes they scare the shit out of me. I think they're coming straight at me."

"You get used to it. I don't even hear them anymore," Alex says.

"Sometimes I'm in my house, it feels like the house is going to shake apart, the windows break, everything," Dennis says.

"Imagine working there. Those guys must be deaf, dude."

"They wear ear plugs or headphones," Rickie says.

No one says anything for a minute.

"You ever flown?" Dennis asks Rickie.

"No."

"Remember?" Alex says to Rickie. "We went to the airport on a field trip in elementary. What, third grade? Miss Fisher? They let us go on a plane and sit down for a minute and put on those big ass headphones. You couldn't hardly hear anything, that's right."

"You ever flown on a plane?" Dennis asks Alex.

"No, I never been out of this place hardly," he says with short sweep of his hand to mean the neighborhood. "Except for driving to T.J. and one time going with my uncle and my mom and sisters all the way to my grandpa's place in Jalisco. That was cool," he says, and Rickie knows Alex is eager to tell them how much he wants to go there to live, that it's his life's dream to go and work on his grandfather's ranch, but he holds up. It's too valuable to throw out into the hot, close air with the stinking cars going by.

"I never flown," Oscar says, anxious to be part of the conversation, "but I been to the beach."

"I been to Santa Monica," Dennis says.

"Dude, you were on that same field trip to the airport," Rickie says to Dennis. "Don't you remember?"

"I was?"

"I been to Santa Monica, too, dude," Oscar says. "The water's dirty there. I thought I was going to get sick just from putting my feet in it."

"Me, too," Dennis says. "You swim?"

"I can't swim."

"M'either. I wouldn't want to swim in that water anyways."

Alex asks Rickie quietly, "Remember that time me and you went?"

"Yeah. I didn't like it. Too much sky and water. Going on forever. It made me feel sick or scared or something."

"It's cooler there."

"It's crazy, dude," Dennis says. "We live like a little bit from there, and we never been and we never go. We stay in this shithole and fry and listen to the planes going off to somewhere we'll never go and those people over there at the beach enjoy all the cool air and the ocean breeze. That's sad, dude. Wait until my dad lets me take the car. I'm going every weekend. Pick up girls and shit." He stops to think about that, and the others nod quietly in agreement.

Oscar stands up.

"Where're you going, dude?" Dennis asks.

"I don't know. My house, I guess. I can't stand it when it gets hot. I'm gonna call Patty. She's got a pool. You want to go over her house?"

"Yeah," Dennis says.

Alex watches Rickie to see what his response will be. "Maybe," he says. "Call me if she says it's okay."

"Me, too," Alex says.

"I'm comin' with you, dude," Dennis says as he gets up from the table and throws the bottle cap into the trash can by the side of the building. He raises his arms in celebration when it goes in. "Two points!"

After they've gone, Rickie and Alex sit without speaking for a while.

"That guy's an asshole," Rickie says finally.

"Who?"

"That guy at the music store. Oscar. My old man. They all piss me off."

Alex says nothing. They both look around and take in the immediate surroundings—the overflowing trash can at the sidewalk, the walls of the restaurant grey from car exhaust, the marred tables and benches, dark splotches of gum ground into the concrete, plastic ketchup packages on the ground with squirts of ketchup hardening in the sun and packs of flies buzzing around; the pawn shop and second-hand store, the *pupuseria* and the old movie theater across and down the street turned into some kind of crazy church.

"This place, dude…"

"What?"

"Look at it. Damn! I feel like I'm finally seeing it. I want to get my mom and sisters outa here. It makes me sick." He pauses for a moment. "It scares me, dude, like it's going to hold on to me and not let me go. D'you know what I mean? You don't want to get out of here, get out of this?" he asks Rickie quietly.

"No. I don't know."

A smoking car putters down the wide boulevard.

"I'd go in a heartbeat if I could get my mom to move back to Mexico. I want to get out of here. Ride horses, help my grandpa on his ranch. When's the last time you been to Mexico?" he asks.

"I never been. My grandma has a sister there." He gets up. Alex carries the trash to the barrel next to the restaurant wall. They walk to the end of the block and across the boulevard back into their neighborhood.

"The people there made fun of my Spanish, laughed when I said things and asked me to repeat them. That sucked," Alex says.

Mailboxes that tilt back or lean on bent pipes toward the street are hand-lettered in black paint that dripped and ran; faded newspapers, hardened black dog shit, paper cups, broken glass at the curbs; curtainless windows, houses painted so long ago that the paint turned to powder and blew away, leaving grey board or naked cinderblock to the relentless sun and wind; but most of all the dirt, the barren hard-packed dirt of backyards under shade trees, the pebbly dirt of the baseball diamond, the fine choking sand carried by the Santa Ana winds that sneaks in beneath sashes and past louvers and coats window sills and dressers and anything left untouched or unmoved for a few days—this is what Rickie knows, what he has come to expect and accept as the real world. Everything else is a fantasy or an unfilled promise. Even if he were to leave it physically, he fears he will end up in a place that looks just like this. Or even if it doesn't, even if his father isn't lying and where he lives the air is clear and the sun bright and the streets clean, Rickie fears that he carries some contagion, some alien seed, that will infect the new place and turn it into this place. He can't leave. What if he finds his vision of people and places to be true? It's better to stay, better not to know for certain.

"See ya," Alex says as he turns off on his block. "I'll call you if I'm going over Patty's. It's going to be too hot."

CHAPTER 16

When Rickie arrives back at his grandmother's house, his father's car is gone, and he is surprised by his feelings about that. Something in him wanted his father still there to press him further about going to Ventura. He's not exactly sure why—either to acquiesce or to fight, maybe some of both.

He goes into his room and slumps down on the end of the bed, finds the remote and turns on his TV. A Dodgers game broadens across the screen. Vin Scully's voice, like the fond voice of a neighbor or relative so familiar that it insinuates itself easily into waking moments and dreams, enters the room. He is in the middle of an anecdote about one of the Arizona players. Rickie almost lets the smile reach his lips as he remembers that he used to imagine himself playing for the Dodgers with Vin talking about him on the air.

"Well, the Dodgers"—he could hear the 'o' the way Vin says it—"young second baseman, Rickie Trujillo, has been quite a story, a home-grown product from the San Fernando Valley. Here's the pitch. Ball, outside. What a find he's been! This youngster has the savvy of a veteran in the field and at the plate. Garcia winds and comes home with the pitch. Trujillo swings and lines a base hit to right, Martinez around second and taking third," Vin would say with that air of amazed inevitability he used when a player proved him right. "I'll tell you folks, this kid is a dandy. He reminds me of..."

Last year, at the end of the season, the coaches treated the team to pizza at Shakey's. The other players ran around or played the video games like little kids, but Rickie watched the game on TV. Coach Vega slid in next to him and watched for a couple of minutes. When he got up to join the other coaches, he put his hand on Rickie's shoulder and leaned in close to be heard over the noise.

"That could be you some day, *mi'jo*. You got a shot." Rickie could finish high school, attend a junior college, maybe Glendale or Pierce, where he would be scouted by Riverside or UCLA, Arizona State or Texas maybe, one of the places with a solid baseball program, and then, who could tell?

"*Orale, mi'jo.* A lot of players come from L.A., from right here in the Valley. You could be the next one."

With a melancholy that grew during the year following that night at Shakey's, Rickie came to realize that other people, anonymous and featureless, would fill the positions on the diamond, not him. He didn't know when he had vacated the scene; he just had.

He changes the channel, bored by the slow pace of the game. Golf. Movies he doesn't recognize. A religious show featuring a woman with impossibly big blond hair and too much make-up and a man with silver hair sprayed in place. They look like Barbie and Ken grown old and weird—someone in school said that, and Rickie marveled how that person could see things like that, could connect things, could see one thing and make it into another. He can't do that. He sees what is, nothing more, nothing less. Korean TV. He checks the Spanish channels. Boxing. He pauses to watch a couple of Mexican lightweights. These little guys never knock each other out, just box and win by decision, *vatos* trying to escape their destiny in whatever *barrios* they live.

The last Spanish channel features a stout, affable host who thinks everything is amusing and worth a laugh, and two beautiful Latinas, one with her hair like a blond aureole, the other with satiny black hair pulled back close to her head, lips so full and alluring, wide smiles, blindingly white teeth, full hips, breasts overflowing their low-cut, tight dresses. Rickie watches them for a while, listens to the playful and sexually charged banter between the host and the two women, and feels himself aroused. They are a fantasy, Phelan said in class one day, a fantasy that makes you go out and buy something because you hope you get the girl if you buy the product. Something like that. And then he said that they were no more real than the religious Barbie and Ken and the young women on MTV, a fantasy that convinced you to send some money or to buy something, or ended up in a wad of tissue, he said. Some of the boys laughed and hooted. Some girls laughed quietly, some whispered to others, who showed they finally got it by blushing. Rickie wonders if everyone feels the crushing emptiness that follows, and the acute awareness of the silence of things in the room, but, of course, he said nothing in class. He thinks briefly of Claudia and yesterday in the deserted house, but that memory makes him uncomfortable.

He turns the TV off and looks at the dead screen in silence.

The phone rings. Claudia. "What's up?" he says.

"Rickie?" she sounds hesitant.

"What's up?"

"Nothing. What's up with you?"

"Just kickin' it."

"Me, too. It's *hot* in my house."

"You want me to come over?"

She hesitates.

"I don't know."

"You got something else planned?"

"Maybe with my mom. Rickie..."

"What happened after I left last night?" he asks, wondering if there had been any fights or shots fired.

"You heard? Oh, shit. I was going to tell you." He hears regret and fear in her voice.

"Heard what?"

"You know. Who told you? Gloria? I told that bitch to keep her mouth shut. Promise you won't be angry?" she wheedles. Rickie says nothing.

"Promise?"

"Okay. Promise. What are you talking about?"

"I was... with one of the security. Gloria was, too. She was worse than me."

When Rickie says nothing, she continues. "He wouldn't leave me alone. He kept after me and after me. I told him about you, but he said he didn't care."

Rickie was going to ask for his name but realizes that she would probably not know it or lie. He tries to empty himself of anger, to feel nothing beyond a cold boredom urging him to hang up. But if he does hang up, that will leave him nothing to do again.

"Where?"

"In his car. He ... It wasn't very long."

"And you couldn't say no."

"I'm sorry, Rickie," Claudia says. She's about to cry.

"Did you do anything else with him?" Without warning, despair flushes through his body as though replacing the blood that runs in his veins. He hears it in his voice. He already knows the answer. Claudia doesn't respond. He doesn't love her, he tells himself, always knew she was too easy, at the same time wonders if she compared their quick and unsatisfying sex in the abandoned house with her time with the security guard and found Rickie wanting.

"Rickie?" she says in a little girl voice.

"You let him..." He doesn't want to give it a name; that will make it too real, too final. His head begins to pound behind his eyes.

"No. He forced me. He wouldn't stop. I tried to make him, I really did. I thought he was going to hurt me if I didn't let him. Oh, Rickie," she wails. For a brief moment, he sees her as a young girl with her arms pinned, forced onto the back seat of a car by a much stronger predator in a black T-shirt who is determined to get what he wants, and he feels a terrible helplessness, for himself and her.

"Did he force you to get in the car?" he asks, but she doesn't respond because she is sobbing.

Like an emphysema patient trying to suck air into damaged lungs, Rickie sits up straight and pulls air in and holds it. He hears Claudia's mother in the background and the call ends. He takes the phone from his ear, still listening for Claudia's despairing cries, but it's silent. He expels the air he has been holding in.

The silence in the room is deep. He feels out of his league, like when he plays a video game whose rules he hasn't bothered to read and whose codes he doesn't know. His characters die quickly and Game Over is displayed on the screen.

When the phone rings, he holds it for a moment, then powers it off. He has nothing to say, no comfort to offer. What has happened to her feels like an inevitability, as though living in this neighborhood makes it so. Not Laugh Now, Cry Later, but Cry Now and Cry Later, an assurance that everything good, every innocent thing will be defaced and defiled, the source of great sadness. The Claudia he knew is lost to him, broken and scattered, and he can do nothing to retrieve her.

He has to escape this feeling.

He stands up and goes to the closet, pulls out a pair of black dress shoes he wears to weddings and funerals. From the inside of one of the shoes, he withdraws a plastic bag with two joints and a package of matches. He takes out one of the joints and the matches and puts the plastic bag back in the shoe and the shoes back in the closet. He walks quietly through the kitchen and checks on his grandmother who is still asleep on the couch. He walks back through the kitchen and out the back door.

The garage is detached from the house. It has two doors, one that faces the side of the house and one in the back. His grandfather added the back door when he converted the garage to a bedroom. Rickie enters by that door and leaves it open.

His brother Bill was the last person to actually live in the room, and his posters of Los Lobos and Poncho Sanchez are still on the walls. They are curling at the top and the bottom. A single bed is pushed up against one wall; a small dresser, a table from a dinette set that their grandfather bought at a yard sale along with a single chair and a pink three-light tree lamp are against the other walls. An oval hooked rug covers most of the exposed floor.

He lived in this room when he was a baby, but he doesn't remember. He wants some memory of comfort and love from his parents, but it is not present. Instead, there's his mother sitting on the couch eating chips and drinking sodas and only reluctantly giving him some after he begs and begs and is pushed away to the other end and cries... And, of his father? Nothing. Zero. A blank. Only whispered conversations between his grandparents at the kitchen table that ceased when he entered the room.

What gave that bastard the right to rape Claudia? What gives his father the idea that Rickie would go live with *him*, make *his* life right by saying everything's okay now? Not in a million years. He can die a lonely old man; Rickie works hard at trying not to care.

It is dark and still and hot in the room, the only light coming from the open doorway and a window that faces the neighbor's wooden fence which has been darkened and made splintery by the winter rains and summer heat. Rickie slides the window open and sits on the edge of the bed. He lights the joint and inhales deeply.

It is as though his body wants to remember, but his mind contracts into a fist that will not release the heightened expectancy, the anticipation aching in his stomach. It will not allow him to remember anything, refuses to think about his father or what has happened to Claudia or baseball or this summer, any of it.

The marijuana begins to take effect. The muscles in his stomach relax like a tangle of snakes unwinding and slithering off in different directions. It is as though his body finally exhales after holding its breath. The familiar sensation overtakes him, of with-drawing from and, at the same time, immersing himself in, the present moment. He focuses on the smooth curve of his nails, their pleasant, almost oily slickness when he rubs his thumb across each surface; the soft, cool skin of his fingers; a dog bark-ing, someone mowing a lawn; the still, dark heat of the room which seems to entomb him. Each sensation comes to him one at a time at a pleasantly reduced speed. He imagines a Pharaoh laid out in his pyramid, deep within a small dark room and safe from thieves and enemies and the demands of his subjects, walled off from the sights and sounds of the world, the room still and dark, maybe with one beam of sunlight from some secret air vent so that he can see—dead, yet aware of everything about him—specks of dust like gold flakes floating in the beam of light. His life has been good. He has been wealthy and powerful, wise beyond his years, a great boy-king whom women young and old adored and desired, and men sought out for his wise counsel.

For a brief moment, he has a vision of himself as someone else, someone powerful and smart, not just Rickie from the neighborhood or Rickie the baseball player, but a different hu-man being completely: living elsewhere, dressing differently in a suit and a shirt and a tie, speaking differently and saying impor-tant things. Rickie feels like he's on the verge of understanding something, something that will give him hope, but a thickness pervades his body, particularly behind his eyes and throughout his limbs, making it hard to think. The thickness gains substance and weight and holds him immobile as he sits on the edge of the bed. He doesn't care. He doesn't fight it. He takes a last hit from the joint, mostly paper now, which causes him to cough until he gags, and then he drops it on the floor and grinds it out with the toe of his shoe. He stares at the scrap of ragged paper and the smudge of ash on the floor; he will have to remember to wipe it up later on. He is tired now. He knows he can sleep deeply, a Pharaoh in this tomb-like room, a welcome sleep like death. Yes, this must be what dying is like, a sort of surrender, a letting-go of all the world's worries, a wall constructed against life that forbids anything to enter and disturb a person any more. Death will be welcome if it is like this, a final relaxation.

He lies on the bed on his back, his head on the slipless pillow, his legs crossed at the ankles, his arms folded across his chest. The boy-king at rest. He smiles at the thought. And in the Sunday quiet of a hot June afternoon, without the roar of planes taking off or landing for the moment, sealed off from the rank smell of the landfill and the other sights and sounds and smells of this neighborhood of poverty and neglect, he is winged off to dreamless sleep on fragile visions of pyramids and Pharaohs lying in state.

CHAPTER 17

When he wakes up in the early evening, it takes him a moment to orient himself, to remember where he is. He sits up and listens. The neighbor is wheeling his trash barrel down the driveway to the curb with a grinding, jarring noise. Trash pick-up tomorrow morning. School. Maltrey. Lopez. Phelan. Claudia trying to explain. Cold-eyed Oscar, waiting impatiently for Rickie to prove himself. Soon his father is going to return and fight with him again about the move to Ventura.

He sits without moving for a moment and waits for those thoughts to vanish. They do not. His stomach rumbles hungrily.

He stands, reaches down to pick up the scrap of paper from the joint and scrapes the spot clean with his shoe. He closes the window and smooths the bed. When he reaches the doorway, he looks back. It looks just as it had been. Every now and then *abuela* dusts and vacuums the room. He does not want her to worry about him using it. He locks the door behind him.

His grandmother is sitting up watching TV.

"Where have you been?"

"Sleeping." He can count on her not to ask too many questions. He sits down heavily in the armchair.

"I thought you were with your friend."

He says nothing. "Where's that man?"

"He went to see Daisy. I think he is going back there tonight," she says, and he knows she means Ventura. "He wants you to go up there to live with him," she says finally.

"I know."

"It's better up there I think."

"I'm not going. I'm staying here."

"Why, Junior? It's no good for you here. Too many bad people. You get in trouble too much."

"I haven't been in trouble for a long time," he lies, affecting an injured tone. Tomorrow she will hear from the school about Maltrey. Lopez will come to the house again, and Rickie will have to go to another school. "No one has called you."

She looks at him for a moment without speaking.

"What is here for you?" she asks finally.

"My friends. My school. My baseball team."

"You can get better friends and a better school," she replies. She does not know about baseball teams.

"I like it here. This is where I belong."

Again she looks at him without speaking. "No, Junior," she says finally, "this is where your grandfather and I could buy, not where I belong or you belong." She pauses. "I do not belong here. I belong home with my sister, Guadalupe. You can come, also, to Mexico, but I think you are too American. You will be unhappy there." She pauses again and looks at him closely, this strange boy with whom she can barely talk. Even when he does speak with her, it is reluctantly and not spoken so much as grunted or mumbled, and almost impossible to understand. She fears that she has lost him.

"This is no place for my good boy," she says, using the words from his childhood. "You belong where the people are nice and the air is good and people take care. Your father is good. He made a mistake, but he was young. He has grown up. He could watch after you and help you and..."

"I don't like him," Rickie says, and adds in English, "He's an asshole." He rises from the chair.

Berta does not know the English, but she recognizes the anger and the disrespect in the tone.

"It is not correct to speak like that," she calls to his back.

"Sorry. I'm hungry," he says as he walks into the kitchen.

"Junior, come here," she commands.

He comes back into the room and stands in a manner that says that the continuation of this conversation is an imposition. She stares at him hard.

"What?" he says, shifting into a neutral stance.

"I brought you up. I made life good for you. Now I am tired. I want to go home before I die. I want to take your grandfather with me and bury him where he belongs."

"You're telling me that I *have* to go live with my father?" he says in English and then in Spanish.

"Don't raise your voice," she says. "I know what is best and this is best for you. Soon I am going to sell this house and move."

"When did you decide this?" He is astounded and hurt by the suddenness of her decision. In an instant, he feels as though he is standing on wind-blown and shifting sand.

"Today. After I spoke with your father. I did not tell him."

"Good, because I'm not going. I'll go live with my friends," he says and leaves the room again.

She lets him go without responding. She sits looking at the worn and faded carpet at her feet, sadly shaking her head.

He goes to the refrigerator and stands with the door open looking in: milk, butter and lard and a few half-full jars and some cans covered with foil. He finds a roll of chocolate chip cookie dough and puts it on the counter, and then searches the lower cabinets for a cookie sheet. By the time he finds one, his grandmother is standing in the doorway.

"What are you doing?"

"I'm going to make cookies," he says without turning to look at her.

"Grease the pan," she says and walks through to her bedroom.

Before he begins, he goes into his room and gets his iPod and headphones.

He slices the dough, places the slices on the sheet he has greased with lard, and sits at the table while they bake. The angry voices and the music are loud in his ears, so loud that his grandmother, who sits on the edge of the bed in her room, can hear it. To her it sounds like people shouting above the sound of a washing machine filling with water at the *lavanderia*. She has warned him that the noise will damage his ears, but he pays no attention.

After the first sheet of cookies has cooled, he sits at the table with a large glass of milk and eats them all, eating and listening to his headphones and trying to quell the rumbling in his stomach and to silence the angry thoughts that race in maddening circles in his mind. His face is hardened, his eyes without movement, staring into the future.

He sits looking out the door to the backyard, but he does not register the light leaving the sky and the deepening nightfall, the heat of the kitchen, the sounds of his grandmother leaving her room to go to the bathroom and return to her room for the night.

In the space of less than a day, the life he has known is gone. She is going to sell this house and move. *He* will have to move to a place he has never even visited, to live with a man he hates, who is a deserter, a betrayer. And his grandmother. She is a deserter as well, willing to abandon him so that she can go live with her sister. And Claudia. Everybody will know by tomorrow afternoon what happened with the security guard at the wedding. Will she even mention Rickie?

He rises abruptly from the table, puts the glass in the sink and the second sheet of cookies on a plate. He has some small notion that finding the cookies there in the morning will appease his grandmother, and perhaps she will reconsider her plans.

He goes into the living room and turns on the TV. He slumps on the couch, the hand with the remote outstretched. He clicks through the channels, looking for anything to capture his interest.

What will he do if his grandmother does sell? Alex. Maybe he can move in with Alex and his mom. No, she doesn't like Rickie. She doesn't say anything, but she doesn't have to. He knows by the cool greeting he receives from her whenever he goes over to their house, the added emphasis she gives to her little speech telling Alex to stay out of trouble any time he and Rickie go off together, and the meaningful parting look she always gives Rickie. She definitely thinks Rickie is trouble. She will never let him stay.

Maybe if he promises, if he pleads the baseball team, finishing high school, the fact that he doesn't really know or like his father—will she listen? Or will she stand at the doorway and tell him she's sorry but no, he's a bad influence, she doesn't trust him?

Night falls as he sits there. The objects in the room recede into shadow. Every now and again, he remembers that this is the time he should get up and set his clothes out for school the next day, take a shower, find some money for lunch, but he doesn't move. He's reached a decision; he isn't going to go to school tomorrow. He has something more important to do, an angry statement to make. He digs his cellphone out of his pocket.

"Alex," he says into the phone.

"Who is this?" Alex says.

"Who do you think, fool."

"Hey. What's up?"

"I'm coming over."

"It's after ten o'clock, dude. Tomorrow's school. I'm about to go to sleep."

"I got a plan."

"What kind of plan? You sound weird. Are you all right?"

"Just meet me at the end of your block. Don't let your mom see you go out," Rickie says and hangs up quickly before Alex can respond.

He walks quietly through the house, out the kitchen door, which he closes tightly behind him, and back into the garage bedroom. He knows a flashlight is in a bracket on the wall by the door because he watched his grandfather install it. He finds it, pulls it off the wall, and turns it on. The light is dim but it works. On the other side of the door in the corner is his grandfather's toolbox. He made it himself, a large wooden box with a hasp in the middle and rope handles on the ends. It is worn on the top, smoothed by Osvaldo using it as a seat while he took a break or ate his lunch. Rickie runs his hand over the smooth wood, and for a moment the thought of his grandfather makes him hesitate and consider going back inside the house and calling Alex to say he isn't coming over. But then he spots the crowbar and feels that it is a sign, an indication of the inevitability of what he is about to do. He picks it up, along with a hammer and a pair of hardened work gloves beneath the hammer. He has what he needs.

Alex is waiting for him at the street corner.

"C'mon, let's go," Rickie says, walking by Alex at a brisk pace.

"Hey, wait a minute. What's going on?" Alex doesn't move.

"We're going back to that place where that racist was," Rickie says. He has stopped and looks back, but has not turned all the way. Alex can't see his face.

"Who're you talking about?"

"That guy who hates Mexicans where we got thrown out of today."

"You mean that stereo store?"

"Yeah. Him. C'mon." Rickie is impatient to get going.

"What are we going to do there?" Alex looks suspiciously at Rickie, moving to his left so that he can better see Rickie's eyes. Rickie turns so that he can't.

"I'm just gonna fuck it up a little bit. Get in, smash some shit, and get out. I'm not going to take anything," he says, thinking that will allay Alex's doubts. "I'm tired of people walking over us, thinking we don't do anything."

"Who're you talking about?"

"It don't matter. Are you coming or not?"

"What do you need me for?" Alex begins to move slowly toward Rickie.

"I don't. Just to come along and watch. On second thought, you don't have to come. Go on home."

"No, I'll go," he says reluctantly.

"Good. C'mon. It'll be cool. Just in and out. I'm going to show that bastard that he can't fuck with us."

The boys walk up the street and then over on to Landerman Boulevard.

At 10:30 on a Sunday night, all of the stores and shops are closed. Even Johnnie's where they ate earlier is dark. Few cars pass on the wide boulevard. A handful of people walk the sidewalks, quickly now, eager to get home.

"We've got to get off this street," Alex says. "If a cop sees us, sees you carrying that stuff, he'll stop us."

"We can cross here," Rickie says and begins to run diagonally across the boulevard. "It's up there," he calls, gesturing with his chin toward a place on the other side of the street, in the middle of the next block. "Not in front," he says. They gain the sidewalk and Alex heads for the store. "In back."

They run down the street, around the corner, and into the alley. It is dark, completely unlit. Dumpsters line the walls.

"Shit," Rickie says quietly. "I didn't bring the flashlight. I don't have my cellphone, either. I must've put them down somewhere."

"How're we going to tell which door it is?" Alex asks. "This is a stupid idea, Rickie."

"Quiet for a minute. Let me think. Was it the third or the fourth store?"

"I don't know," Alex says. "I don't like it, Rickie. We can't see nothing."

"I know. Do you have your cell?"

"No, I left it on the bed."

They don't speak for a moment. Rickie is waiting for his eyes to grow more accustomed to the poor light. In the silence they hear a scrabbling noise coming from the dumpster nearest them.

"What the hell is that?" Alex asks in a loud whisper.

"Quiet, dude! You'll get us caught. It's probably a cat or a *ratón* looking for food."

Alex steps away from the dumpster and eyes it suspiciously.

"I got to take a leak," he says.

"Go ahead, piss on the dumpster. I'm going to find out which door is his."

Rickie heads for the nearest door as Alex relieves himself, the sound of the urine splattering on the ground amplified by the near walls and metal dumpsters. Rickie checks a further door.

"This is it," he calls in a loud whisper. "Come here."

Alex picks his way as quickly as he can in the darkness. When he gets to the door, they peer in past the wrought iron bars that cover the glass on the inside. They can see the counter, the stacks of boxes silhouetted against the blue light of the boulevard coming in at the front window display and door, latticed by a metal gate drawn across the width of the store.

"This *pendejo* should put in better security back here," Rickie says. "Here, hold these." He hands Alex the hammer and crowbar and puts on the gloves. He grabs the crowbar. Alex takes a step back.

From the moment Rickie sticks the tongue of the bar between the door and the frame and gives it a sharp pull, the alarm begins to sound.

Alex is ready to run. "C'mon, let's get out of here." He can't keep the fear out of his voice.

"Not yet," Rickie yells, liberated by the racket of the alarm. "I'm gonna do some damage."

The door, however, is made of metal, as is the frame. The most he does is crush the edge of the door where the crowbar has been angled. The metal creases, the paint chips, but the locks hold.

"Shit," he yells after one last yank on the crowbar. He holds it in both hands like a baseball bat and slams it against the door repeatedly.

Alex slaps him on the shoulder. "C'mon, we got to get out of here. The cops'll be coming," he yells.

Rickie turns on him. "Leave me the fuck alone," he shouts. Alex recognizes the look in his eyes. He lets his hand fall, holds both arms out as though in surrender, and begins to back off.

"I'm going, fool. I'm not sticking around," he yells. Alex turns and begins trotting out the way they came in. He throws the hammer he still holds into one of the dumpsters. The alarm reverberates insistently in the narrow alley. Dogs bark. Lights go on in buildings on the other side of the wall. Someone comes into the alley at the far end and stands looking down toward them.

Rickie becomes aware of the futility of continuing to strike the door, and he follows Alex out of the alley. He catches up with him halfway down the block on Landerman. Alex begins to run faster.

"We've got to get off this street. They'll see us for sure," Alex calls back as he runs.

"Go down to Sycamore Way," Rickie shouts back. Sycamore Way is a wide east-west street that goes all the way across the Valley floor. When they reach the intersection, they stop.

"Come here," Alex says. "Get out of the light." He stands in the shadow of a doorway. Rickie stands at the curb, bent over and trying to get a deep breath and looking up and down the street. He looks back at Alex but doesn't move.

On the south side of the street are low industrial buildings behind high chain link fences topped with coiled razor wire. No chance there. On their side of the street and on the next couple of blocks west of them, there are apartment complexes behind low fences mixed in with a tool store, a *lavendaria*, and an adult video rental shop.

"Which way?" Rickie says, still bent over and looking back at Alex. "Do you know anyone in those apartments?" he asks Alex when he finally gets his breath. "Think."

"I can't think, dude. You think." Alex is angry and scared. "Get away from the street. Don't you hear the freakin' sirens?" Finally, Rickie moves into the shadow of the doorway.

They stand without speaking. Rickie races through his memory in an attempt to recall who lives in one of the apartments along Sycamore Way. No one comes to mind. He has actually never been inside an apartment there. It strikes him in a moment of fleeting self-pity and wonder how few friends he has. A lot of people nod or say hi to him in the hallways at school, but almost all of them keep a safe distance from him. Rickie moves closer to the doorway.

"We can't stay here," Alex says. "They'll be shining every doorway. We've got to get into the neighborhood and back home."

"That house. The abandoned house. We can stay there until it calms down." The house is about five blocks north of where they are. They both look up the long stretch of Landerman they will have to cover.

"We'll never make it. It's too far. Let's cross here and try to get home," Alex says. They run across the boulevard and into the sleeping neighborhood.

CHAPTER 18

When the call comes in, one car is dispatched to check it out—Officer Adrian Sanchez, who has just begun his thirteenth year on the force, and his partner, Officer Chris Padilla, who has six months on the job. They have been at the park about a half a mile away rousting a haggard young white woman and her eight-year-old son in a battered Ford station wagon. She is dressed in a dirty UCLA hooded sweatshirt and a long thin skirt and beat-up boots. Her blond hair is stringy and matted, and her face gaunt.

"Where? My parents are dead, I got no family, my old man beats me up and hits the kid if he tries to protect me. Every time I find a place he hunts me down like it's the only thing he's got to do in his miserable life. Where? Where am I going to go? Do you know how long we've been living like this?" She leans against her car, holding up her hand to shield her eyes from the spotlight shining from the police car. She positions herself to block the light from hitting the boy sitting sleepily in the back seat wrapped in a large towel he uses as a blanket. The towel is dirty and tattered.

"There's a shelter up on..." Officer Sanchez begins.

"I been there. That's where he found us last time."

"Haven't you got any friends?" the young cop ventures naively.

The woman snorts. "Yeah. The other homeless I meet panhandling at 7-Eleven. Not friends exactly. They don't want to see me. I might get something they don't get. We talk anyways. Misery loves company," she says disdainfully. "Can you shut that light off or move it out of my face and off the kid? The kid has got to get some sleep. I send him to school, you know."

Sanchez motions with a quick nod of his head to Padilla. "Turn it off." He turns on a flashlight, which he points at their feet.

"Well, ma'am, you can't stay here in the park. City ordinance. We'll be back in a while. I don't want to find you here," Sanchez says and begins to walk back to the car. "Try to find a space on the street."

"Where am I supposed to find that? Every space is taken," she says, knowing that these two don't have an answer.

Padilla shuts off the spotlight and comes back and surveys the scene, now lit only by the flashlight and the nearby street lights.

"Good luck," he says.

"C'mon, Padilla, we have to answer that call," Sanchez says as he stands at the open car door.

Padilla turns to join his partner.

They drive north on Landerman, pull a U-turn in front of the store and shine the spotlight on the door and display window.

"Nothing here," Padilla says.

They drive around in back.

Officer Padilla gets out and shines his flashlight on the alley door. "Yeah, they tried to get in here," he calls. "Lot of damage to the door, but they didn't get in."

"Probably kids. Stupid. Can't even do it right. C'mon. Let's see if they're still around." Padilla gets in and they drive slowly up the alley shining the spotlight and the flashlight into the darkened doorways and by the dumpsters. At the end of the alley, they turn left into the neighborhood.

"What time is it?" Sanchez asks. His vest is digging into him. He ate too much dinner and doesn't feel well. He wants to lie down, and then wake up with the energy and enthusiasm he once felt. He envies Padilla.

Padilla lights the face of his watch. "Almost midnight."

Sanchez curses. "I could've swore it was later. It's going to be a long night," he sighs. "I didn't sleep good this morning. Kids making too goddam much noise. I hate trying to sleep weekends." He yawns noisily as though to make his point.

In this particular area, it's as though the mapmaker was left with only ends of streets or short pieces, and finding empty spots, had placed them down haphazardly. Or as if he had laid out the grid with pencil and had erased it in a number of places and had then been called away, never to return and make sense of the work. Only Sycamore Way runs east to west all the way through to the next major street; Landerman is the only north-south line. In the crazy quilt of the neighborhood west and north of these boulevards, streets run a block or two and end. Without warning, one street becomes a narrow path skirting an overgrown field. People grow frustrated when they drive the short streets and realize the piece they are seeking picks up on the other side of a barrier or a block beyond a cul-de-sac.

At night this neighborhood is cast in darkness. No street-lights illuminate the way. On a moonless night like this, with a haze of leftover smog smothering the starlight and the ambient city light, the darkness is almost palpable.

Sanchez and Padilla cruise the neighborhood on the west side of Landerman, shining the spotlight into yards and on doorways and gates, causing dogs to bark and cats to scurry across the street and the few people still awake to look out living room windows. The officers find no one.

"If we don't find anyone, we'll go on the other side," Sanchez says. "This is like looking in one of them puzzles."

"Like a maze?"

"Yeah. And we're the rats," Sanchez says and glances over at his young partner to see if he appreciates his attempt at humor. Padilla smiles. What a shame, the older cop thinks. Seen from this side, his partner is a handsome guy. Women would look again; that's what Sanchez's wife had said. But on the other side is that ugly raised scar that runs from the corner of his mouth to his eye. When they see it without expecting it, people pull back in shock. Poor Padilla—his own father going after him with a broken bottle as the boy tried to protect his mother.

"If they're anywhere," Sanchez says, turning away from his thoughts, "they're probably behind a bush in back of those ugly brown apartments. What a dump. They should bulldoze the whole place with the trash that lives there inside."

"Then they'll all be in the park," Padilla says.

"Yeah, right. Let's go on the other side for a bit. If we don't see nothin', we'll give it up. I'm not going to beat the bushes for them. I feel like shit. I hate Sundays," Sanchez says.

They cross Landerman. On the east side of the boulevard,

the streets are laid out in a complete grid and easier to traverse. Sanchez picks up speed, sure that they will find nothing, eager to get back to the new station and its comfortable bathroom. He can kill at least a half-hour there if nothing else comes up.

"I think I see something. Up there on the right," Padilla says.

"Got'em," Sanchez says and speeds up.

"Two of them. One's taking off."

"Get out and cuff the one standing there. What's he got in his hand?"

"Pry bar."

"Dumb shit. Doesn't even know to get rid of it. Jesus." Sanchez bumps against the curb, headlights in the kid's face. Padilla opens the door and squats behind it, gun drawn and the beam of his flashlight in the kid's face as well. "Drop it! Now! Get your hands up."

The crowbar hits the sidewalk with a loud metallic clang that echoes along the street. Padilla stands.

"This is that kid," he says, relieved and disappointed, "the baseball player. I got'm. Go get the other."

He closes the door behind him, and Sanchez speeds around the corner. Sanchez glances in the mirror. The kid should be on the ground, he thinks; Padilla should have the kid on the ground.

Sanchez watches the taller, darker one take off running. *Moreno*, a gang-banger with his Dickies and his pressed T-shirt and black Nikes, and dreams of power and intimidation quickly turning to ashes. He doesn't say anything to the punk he's with; he just runs, hoping to make it around the corner on to the next block, searching for something to hide behind, a building, a tree, or a fence to stand between him and the inevitable arrest. Fools like this: they always have some outlandish dream secreted away behind the tough talk and the surliness and arrogance. Playing in the NBA. Owning a top-of-the-line BMW or a Mercedes to blow down the 134 Freeway. Being another Scarface bathed in money and diamonds and hot women. Sanchez watches as the kid's feet pound the sidewalk awkwardly and too slowly and almost trip over one another in his haste to find some refuge, and he wonders what hope this one has dared to lock away and hold on to, what light shining in the distance making life tolerable in this god-awful place of poor houses and run-down apartment buildings and dirt and trash and so many faces with a beaten, lonely, lost look. The boy runs as fast as his legs will propel him, but it is fruitless; he's not fast enough to outpace the car or the harsh spotlight or the shit that awaits him.

"¿*Qué pasa, amigo*? What are you and your buddy doing tonight?" Officer Padilla asks as he approaches Rickie. "Turn around. Put your hands behind your back. Interlock your fingers."

Rickie keeps his face averted. If the officer saw the emptiness there, the complete lack of fear, he would make Rickie get down on the ground flat on his face and would cuff him quickly and stand off.

Rickie wonders why the officer is not telling him to get on his knees or on the ground and wait to move in until his partner returns. Maybe it's the fact that Rickie and the cop's brother both play baseball in the park league that makes the cop relaxed and off-guard; Rickie expects that Padilla will start talking about that commonality in some sort of genial way. Anger begins to grow and expand within Rickie. Maybe the man sees himself as a teenager, remembers those days when he acted tough but really wasn't, and he'll chuckle at the remembrance of those days. The anger continues to grow. He's frustrated that they didn't get into the electronics store and didn't have the chance to punish the dismissive owner... frustrated by the fact that this guy with his ugly, smiling scar keeps coming into Rickie's life, trying to be buddy-buddy... angered by Oscar's mere presence pressing Rickie to do something he doesn't want to do... infuriated with his so-called father who showed up out of nowhere and wants to take Rickie away... blinded by his desire for revenge on the security in his tight black T-shirt and his careless superiority and dominance.

When the officer reaches for his cuffs and holsters his weapon, the boy turns and reaches with both hands for it. As he struggles with Padilla for control, Rickie knows that Sanchez is going to yell at his young partner, dress him down good for not following standard procedure.

Officer Padilla has not counted on the boy's quickness or strength. When Padilla looks deep into the boy's face as they grapple for the service weapon and sees the anger registered there and the frightening, grim determination, surprise and fear jump to Padilla's eyes. And in that moment, both of them know someone is going to get hurt.

The weapon's discharge knocks Rickie back on his heels. It is as though he is caught inside the explosion, inside a bubble of sound that slows all actions into discrete pieces. It's as though he sees the bullet enter the young policeman's face under the chin and throw his head back and exit the back of the head in an expulsion of blood and bone, brain tissue, hair and skin.

Rickie stands and watches in horror as the life drains out of the officer's astounded eyes, watches him slump to the ground. He's the wrong one, his mind shouts. Not this cop—the security at the gate, the one who raped Claudia, that one. Oscar. His father. The anger raging within Rickie just a few seconds before has completely evaporated and been replaced by the awful realization that he has made a mistake, that everything here is wrong. His body is washed over by an unexpected sadness, like a blush of fever, and a sense of aloneness he has not felt before. He stares at the dying man, hoping desperately for the eyes to focus and blink or the hands to reach for his face, but nothing.

Officer Sanchez has returned; he has stopped his car in the middle of the street down from Rickie. He yells from behind his open car door for Rickie to freeze. The voice is loud and scared. Rickie wants to stand in silence and understand the enormity of what he has done and his strange feelings, but he knows can't. He wheels around and stares at the man and observes in the snail-like movement of time and action that Alex is in the back seat of the car with his hands behind his back, his head raised in order to see, and a horrified expression on his face as he looks from the fallen policeman to Rickie and back again.

Sanchez fires his weapon. Rickie hears the bullet whistle by his right shoulder and head. And then another. Their deadly whisper brings him completely out of this nightmare and into a more frightening one. Fear and horror pulse through his body and drive his legs to carry him up the street into the darkness.

CHAPTER 19

ickie knows that Coach Vega lives somewhere in the neighborhood. He doesn't really know where. The players on the
team never go there, though somebody said he saw the coach
outside one day but was too shy to stop and say anything. Rickie
can't even remember if the kid said whether it was a house or an
apartment. It won't be fancy, Rickie knows, just a place for a guy
and his wife. Rickie has no idea what street the coach's place is
on; at this point, in his panic and desperation, he can't remember
what street he's currently running on. He's simply looking for a
welcoming light, a haven from the tide of fear carrying his feet
along. He can't get the cop's bewildered and somehow sadly disappointed last look out of his mind. It would have been better if
the cop had cursed his soul to Hell.

Rickie turns a corner and sees a lighted window ahead of him.
Maybe, by some miracle, it's Coach Vega's place. Light falls from
the window onto the brittle grass and dirt. Someone is awake.

The fact that light pours out a window and that a door is open fills Rickie with reckless hope. He runs into the room and stands before the man seated in an armchair reading his paper. It takes Rickie a few seconds to realize that the man seated before him is not Coach Vega. He's a white man with a round freckled face and thinning red hair.

Bewildered and fearful, Rickie stands in front of the man and is surprised by his calm.

"What do you want?" he asks.

"Is Coach here?" the boy asks, looking around the apartment wildly.

"Is *who* here?"

"You got to help me, man. I'm in real trouble. Please."

"What's going on? Is someone chasing you?" the man asks and looks at the open door as he does so; he has become fearful himself, convinced that there's something real and dangerous just seconds away.

"I'll call the cops," he says and reaches for the phone on the TV table next to his chair.

Rickie watches the man as he dials 911and knows a number of things simultaneously: he will never find Coach Vega's house; the cops already know what has happened and are on their way into the neighborhood; he has to get out of here; and he is alone as he has never been before. He knows he's going to die, tonight or tomorrow or the next day. Cops don't allow a cop killer to live, and they will be out by the hundreds, are already mobilizing the helicopters and dogs and whatever else they will need to find him. The night will come alive any minute with sirens and barking dogs, police radios, helicopter rotors chopping the air, and curious neighbors at windows and doors and clustered in yards to hear of this latest disaster to strike the neighborhood.

"Stay here, kid," the red-haired man says to the frightened boy. "I'll get through in a minute. Close the door and lock it. I'll get the blinds."

Rickie stands in the middle of the room indecisively. The cops can't kill him if he just stays here. He'll just lie down on the floor with his hands behind his back and let them cuff him; tell them it was a mistake, he hadn't meant to kill the cop, that he knew him and liked him—he'll exaggerate the truth—never meant to hurt him, just wanted to get away. They can't do anything to him if he gives up.

Yes, they can. They can take him somewhere in the neighborhood, the field by the apartment complex, take the cuffs off, no, not take the cuffs off, but make him run like he's trying to escape and shoot him down like a dog. If they can do what they've done to so many others, they can just as easily kill him. This guy will say they took him away in cuffs; that's all he'll know, nothing else.

"Can you come with me?" Rickie asks.

"Where to?"

"When they take me."

"Tell me what's going on. I don't really understand." The man has pulled the blinds and heads for the open door.

"Don't. Please." Rickie begins to back toward the doorway.

"Okay." The man stops. "Isn't someone chasing you?"

"I can't stay." No, he won't make it easy for them even though he knows the inevitable ending, has known it in some sort of way for a long time. What a strange thing to know—that he will die in this neighborhood. He knew it all along! That's it, that's why, when Lopez asked him to think of himself at twenty years old, at twenty-five, he never had any ideas. All he had seen was a dark screen.

He wants to say something to his coach. "Tell Coach," he begins, as though this man might miraculously find a way to get in touch with Coach Vega. But time is short and it's impossible for Rickie to think of what to say, except that baseball was good and he was a good coach because he cared about his players.

"Tell him what, kid? Tell the coach what?" the man asks, still standing near the door. Then he realizes who Rickie is. "Wait. You're that baseball player. I saw you play. I go to the field to see if your team is playing. You've got skills, dude."

"I'm sorry, mister," Rickie says and pushes past him and bolts out the door. The man goes after him.

"Wait, stay here. It can't be that bad. I can help," he yells after the retreating boy. He follows him out the door to the sidewalk and then tracks the dark figure as he runs up the block and disappears. The first sounds of sirens and helicopters fill the darkness.

Rickie runs wildly up and down darkened streets, across yards, into cul-de-sacs and out again, all the time aware of the mounting noise of sirens and helicopters. He has to get across Landerman, he has to find a place to hide, but in his panic, he has no idea where he is, just that he is on the wrong side of Landerman. It will be too easy to find him here, the streets too regular, too like a checkerboard. The sky all around him will soon be lighted with bright beams probing the streets and yards. The neighborhood that he thought he knew so well in daylight is like a closed door to him now. Tonight and forever, he has no grandfather's hard hands to pat his back or whiskery cheek to lie against his. Tonight, all doors are locked.

Stop. He has to stop and find himself. Which way is Landerman? To his left. How far away is he? He has to look at houses. He knows this place, has spent all of his seventeen years here walking on the streets back and forth to school and friends' houses and the park. He knows street names; he knows faces he has seen working in the yards or beneath the hoods of cars. He knows the wrought iron at windows and the metal security doors and the chain link fences that keep angry dogs at bay. He just has to stop and look.

He stops and turns to look over his shoulder, and in that moment he sees a beam of light pointed toward the ground traveling hurriedly across the night sky as though being dragged against its will to point out the fallen officer and the pool of blood cooling beneath him. Oh, God, Rickie remembers again, I killed a cop. They don't forgive you for that. They kill you. No. He can't think about that. He has to get a hold of himself and figure out how to get across Landerman without anyone seeing him.

He runs north through the neighborhood, thinking it will be better to cross above the electronics store. Maybe they haven't closed it off yet. When he has run until his lungs burn, he heads to his left. Now he moves carefully as he approaches the lighted boulevard. He checks the houses and the yards on his side of the street; he will only have a few seconds to dive for cover if a police car turns onto the street with its searchlight on.

He gets off the broken sidewalk and runs cautiously across the edges of front yards. Most porch lights are off, but he has to fear motion sensing lamps hung from the corners of roofs, snapping on in a glare of blue-white light. If he can only get across Landerman, he'll be all right. He can't think why that is true, but he knows he'll remember once he gets across.

He hears the approaching sirens and stops and crouches down on the grass. It was watered that afternoon. The moisture soaks his pants at the knees. He puts his hands over his head and crouches in a ball to make himself smaller. He knows it will do no good. The siren draws closer and closer. At any moment he expects to see the street in front of him or in back of him brightly lit by headlights, and the car slamming to a stop and cops piling out with guns drawn. He waits.

Two police cars race up Landerman with their sirens blaring, a block away. Rickie raises his head just in time to see the red and blue lights swinging across the building facades as they disappear north on the boulevard. He wipes his wet pants at the knees and takes a number of deep breaths. Somehow, the passing cars give him renewed hope and courage. He walks on the sidewalk again, standing straight up. In back of him the street is clear. In front of him, just a few feet away, is Landerman. He reaches the corner. He has been smart to come up this far. On his left is a *lavandería*, closed now for the night, some dim night light illuminating the dingy walls and the dark hulks of the empty washers and dryers. On his right is the *Iglesia del Valle*, an old movie theater that used to be called *The Landerman* turned into a church.

Coach Vega and some of the other coaches remember it as a movie theater when they were about the age of their players. The coaches laugh conspiratorially the way adults do when they think they know something or when they have something to talk about they don't want kids to hear. Rickie and some of the others laughed at the coaches—dude, they should see what goes on in the back of the theaters *these* days! Yet, at the same time, Rickie wanted to hear, wanted to hear his coach talk about anything that happened to him when he was growing up; wanted to know what he felt, what he did, what he thought about, what confused him or made him happy. Lenny Allen, the only black player on the team, said, "C'mon, man, tell us about it. Shit, what you say ain't going to be nothing we ain't heard before. Or maybe done," and then he laughed and high-fived a kid sitting next to him. Lenny's family had recently moved from South L.A. But Coach Vega, who was sitting on the other side of him, had nudged him gently in the ribs and told him to watch his language and had stood up and told them all they were too young and laughed. They never did hear.

Now the old movie theater marquee, with *The Landerman* still scripted in lights above it, advertises the end of the world. Rickie walks slowly near the dark brick wall of the movie theater and is comforted by the darkness and shadow of the building. The lights on the marquee are off—are they ever lit these days? he wonders—and he runs around to the front of the building and hides in the shadow of the detached ticket booth at the edge of the sidewalk. He wants to see inside it, but the windows are plastered with the same flyers that are in the glass-fronted display boxes, which used to advertise the current feature. The flyers advertise traveling ministers who will be preaching at the church. The most recent one is from two months before.

The thunderous noise of a helicopter crossing overhead brings him back to the present moment. There's no traffic on the boulevard. He looks to his left, down Landerman, and sees a swarm of cop cars with their lights flashing in front of the electronics store. Nothing to his right. Where have those two cop cars gone with their sirens blaring and lights flashing? Is something else going on tonight, too? Something just as bad? Maybe a shootout, *Sol Trece* or 18th Street and the cops? Maybe they'll be blamed for Padilla's death.

He'll have to run across the boulevard. There is a crosswalk but no light. He will have to time it and run when the traffic is clear both ways. He edges out to the curb. Nothing to his right. Nothing to his left. He begins to run. He is about five steps into the crosswalk when a cop car turns a distant corner and heads toward him. Oh, Jesus! Rickie stops and begins to back up slowly. The cop car is now two blocks from the intersection. Have they seen him? It is dark here, the streetlight at the corner blinking off and on sporadically. He backpedals slowly to the curb, stumbles up onto it—shit, the awkward movement will call attention to him—and backs into the darkness of the theater entrance, behind the ticket booth. The cop car reaches the stop sign. Rickie can hear his own breathing like waves crashing the shore. The cops stop momentarily and then cross the street slowly. They're coming for him. They know they have him trapped, so they don't have to hurry. Where is he going to go? Out into the open where they can gun him down? The bright light on the driver's side snaps on and sweeps across the theater entrance. Rickie inches around the opposite side of the ticket booth. The light hits the windows and concrete at his feet, just catching the tip of his Nike. He pulls it back carefully out of the pool of light. If they stop and get out, he's dead.

They pause at the intersection now, not twenty feet away, while the light probes the area between the ticket booth and the doors to the theater. Rickie can hear their radio going nonstop, a woman, but he can't understand anything other than the controlled urgency in her voice. He waits to hear a car door open. That will be his signal to take off across the street no matter what's coming. Sweat runs down his sides. He is aware of his own sour smell.

The light shuts off and the car accelerates into the neighborhood. Rickie steps from behind the ticket booth, takes one quick look both ways on Landerman and sprints across the wide and empty boulevard, up the street from Johnnie's where they ate just this afternoon, feeling the exhilaration and joy of a long distance runner in sight of the finish line. He laughs out loud as he enters the darkened neighborhood west of the boulevard.

CHAPTER 20

When he stops running, he's at the edge of the large empty lot. It isn't fenced, but no kids come over here to play. It's vacant except for the weeds that someone cuts down once each year and the bottles and cans and condoms and fast food containers that people throw out of their cars. Rickie glances up at the power lines crossing it, held up by the tall metal stanchions that scared him as a little boy because they looked like skeletal robots. He used to believe that if he stared long enough, they would begin to move. He still never looks at them for long when he passes by. As he glances up at them now, dark forms against the lighter sky, he feels uneasy in the pit of his stomach and looks away.

If they are in front of him, then Anthony's house must be on his right. Anthony was an elementary school friend who has since disappeared. Rickie recognizes the cinder block fence and the broken blocks where a drunk driver crashed into it. The bougainvillea does not completely cover the damage. So, if this is

Anthony's house, the wedding was at a house just a few blocks over. And beyond that... Now he knows where he is and where he is going.

He runs north a long block until he can go no further. Now to his left. He runs across the street and past an old beige two-story apartment building with tin foil on the windows to the cluster of small, one-story houses. The one sitting furthest from the curb and in the deep shadow of a leafy tree is the abandoned house. The heavy shade, the protection it gives from probing search-lights, provides hope. Maybe they won't find him. They could go right past the house and not even notice it, hidden as it is back from the street in the darkness.

He runs along the side of the house as quickly as he can without making noise, careful to avoid the shards of broken glass on the driveway. Is the garage unlocked? He doesn't stop to find out.

What if someone is there? What if a couple of *vatos* are smoking a blunt or cutting cocaine or tagging the wall? What if he comes across a couple like Claudia and himself? They'll yell, alert the neighbors, maybe even attack him. He'll have to run again, and then where?

For the third time in the last two days, he pushes open the back door of the abandoned house; he stands on the threshold listening. If anyone else is in the house, they have heard him and are listening as well, maybe pulling a gun or a knife or a screwdriver out of a pocket, slowly and quietly rising to their knees, readying to attack. Rickie's heart pounds in his ears. It is unbearably loud, deafening, until he separates it from the other hammering noise, a helicopter nearly overhead. He can see the light grow outside, as though a frightening full moon has suddenly risen. For a brief second, it makes him think of Halloween and being young, no, not young so much as free of fear, like he was only an hour ago. His stomach aches with longing. His eyes well and his throat thickens.

Sirens rise and fall relentlessly in the thick night air, stop suddenly, and then begin again just as suddenly and draw closer. The light from the helicopter comes nearer. He can't stand in the doorway or he'll be spotted. He has to get inside no matter who's there.

He steps into the kitchen.

"Hey," he whispers loudly. "It's okay. I just need a place to hide."

He stops and listens as closely as he can, considering the noise outside and within his own body. He expects to hear a slight shift in position, a leg or arm rubbing on fabric, a shoe scraping the floor. No response. The sound of his whispered words carries into the emptiness and comes back mournfully, as though spoken by a ghost. The skin on his neck and arms prickles with fear. He *has* to move.

He stands at the kitchen door holding his breath, and then begins tip-toeing quietly through the kitchen, past the dining room and down the short hall, past two bedrooms and a bathroom on his left and into the empty living room at the front of the house. Nothing. No people. No furniture. Just darkness. Angular shadows soften and disappear as the light comes closer again. The helicopter is circling overhead. Where is he going to hide? In a bedroom behind a closed door? That's ridiculous.

The helicopter passes overhead again, the beam of light sweeping over the little house and illuminating it with an eerie silver light. He goes up and down the hallway again looking in bedrooms and into the bathroom. Nowhere to hide. Empty rooms with nothing even to hide behind.

Maybe there is some place outside behind a bush or a tree.

No. A crawlspace, maybe, under the house. He imagines rats and spiders, earwigs, roaches, himself lying on dusty cobwebby ground, more fearful of the rodents and the insects than the cops. Crawlspace. Some houses have attics. His grandmother's house has one. There is an access panel to it right in the hallway. Rickie leaves the bedroom he's standing in and goes into the hallway. He looks up. There it is, a small hatch cut into the hallway ceiling.

Except that he can't reach it. The access door is a good couple of feet beyond the reach of his outstretched hand. He will have a chance if he gets up there and hides, but how?

He steps quietly from room to room again, hoping he has missed something to stand on, but the rooms are completely empty. He stands in the kitchen and looks out the door at the backyard, aware of a car going by the front of the house—is it a cop car?—and the relentless hammering of the helicopters.

He realizes what his gaze is resting on—the garage. He knows there is no hiding there, but maybe a step stool or a ladder leaning against a wall, even a rickety chair, anything to boost him up into the attic. He listens. He hears no voices, no sirens. The helicopter heads west in a wide circle. Are the cops on foot searching door to door? He calculates his chances. He doesn't think he can leave this house. He pictures himself running away, running, running, right into a hail of bullets tearing at his clothes, at his flesh, at his face; sees himself shredded by thousands of bullets until the vision becomes so real that he cries out in the dark and empty house. He hadn't meant to kill the cop. He had just been angry, about what he could no longer remember, but angry in a way that blinded him. Again, he wonders if he has a problem in his head, a tumor or something. He has seen a show on television about people with brain tumors who went into fits of rage and did things they did not remember afterwards. But he remembers with terrible clarity that shocked look on the cop's face, which seemed to say that nothing like this should have happened, that Rickie has violated the rules of the game and ruined everything for everybody. Rickie isn't angry now. He is young and helpless and scared. He has to find a place to hide until they give up and he can sneak back home to his room and his bed.

He has to chance running out the back door and hope the garage holds something he can use to climb on. He opens the back door. The yard is cast in bright light and patches of leafy shadow; the air is still. He strains to hear. Maybe they are sneaking up on him now, the cops, not any cops but members of the anti-gang unit. A new fear jolts his body. He has heard stories about them, how they plant drugs or knives or guns on you, the guns with the serial numbers filed off, and take sadistic glee in beating the shit out of you or killing you. And nothing ever happens to them. He has heard of homies who had served years for crimes they didn't commit, and, once released, were visited by these cops at their apartments or little houses in Pacoima or Sylmar and were shown another "clean" weapon or enough drugs to put them away for years. "Why don't you go home to Mexico, leave town, before we find you in possession of something like this, *amigo*?"

These guys are ruthless, and everyone on the street knows it.

The night is frightening in its stillness, as though a hundred sets of eyes watch him, wait for him to expose himself before guns begin to blaze. Fighting the fear that rises in his throat like acid, Rickie edges quietly down the back steps and waits for a moment on the bottom step. The garage is across the small yard with a door on the side facing him. Rickie forces himself to move slowly toward it, stepping on the smooth rock pathway through the narrow garden.

The door is unlocked. Maybe God is with him. Maybe the *Virgén* will protect him from heaven because she knows that, though he has made a terrible mistake, he is young and can be forgiven.

He tries to think of what he has done to warrant divine intervention. All he can think of is that he loves his grandmother. But they fought yesterday. No, not yesterday, this afternoon. He has been a good friend to Alex, but Alex is under arrest and maybe dead because of him.

He stands just inside the doorway of the darkened garage, leaving the door open to allow the ambient light to enter. He turns his head quickly because he thinks he hears voices and the crackle of a police radio. He remains completely still and listens in the darkness. Nothing. No noise except for voices and laughter coming from a nearby TV.

He exhales. Urgency surges through him. He has to find something. He peers into the dark interior. The warm air within is suffused with the smell of gasoline and mowed grass and the hint of paint and paint thinner, a pleasant nostalgic smell for Rickie because it reminds him of the tool shed in the back yard of his grandmother's house where his grandfather stored the mower and the gardening tools and buckets of paint.

One time, when Rickie was a little boy, he ran into the shed during a sudden downpour and laid down in the little bit of space between the mower and the paint cans lined neatly against the wall and stacked two high. He found the pile of old towels that his grandfather used to clean with, spread one on the dry concrete floor, used two as a pillow and another with which to cover himself. It was dry and dark, but not too dark, and the air was a cocktail he associated warmly with the jobs his grandfather performed—mowing the lawn, touching up some wall or woodwork of the house, raking the grass cuttings and Eucalyptus leaves and bark that the neighbor's tree shed when the wind blew. Rickie, the six-year-old boy, fell asleep in that shed and wakened later when his grandfather called for him in the backyard.

"Did you make yourself a bed? Were you sleeping, my child?" his grandfather asked. When Rickie nodded yes, his grandfather laughed and took the little boy's hand in his own hardened hand and led him into the house, where he told Rickie's grandmother what had happened. She was happier in those days, and she laughed, too. Their eyes narrowed when they smiled or laughed and the lines that formed at their temples were like rays of light.

Rickie can see nothing inside from the doorway. He will have to step into the darkness and feel along the walls. He moves to his right and proceeds carefully, his right shoulder bumping against the exposed studs. He forces himself to breathe regularly and with as little noise as possible.

He thinks his best chance is at the back of the garage but it is deep in shadow, so dark as to be almost alive. Maybe something will spring out at him when he gets close, like the shadows in the old movie *Ghost* that carry away the souls of the dead bad guys, but he isn't dead, so it will scare him even more when these shadows jump out at him and grab him and begin to drag him, still alive, toward Hell.

He stops in his tracks. His breath comes in gulps. His heart is pounding and his shaven head, when he puts his hand up to it, is covered in cold sweat. He moves forward again, slowly and sideways, with his right hand thrust in front into the glob of darkness. He inches along until his hand jams against the back wall, stubbing his fingers. The wall is smooth. He lays his palm against the cool smoothness—it's pegboard. He can see it in his mind's eye—the smooth brown material with holes in it for hooks from which you hang tools. Alex's mom has it on a wall in their garage, but there are only a few hooks stuck in the holes and nothing hangs from them.

He leans against the back wall. He can't stay here. One cop with a flashlight will be able find him. He has to go back inside the house and hide in a closet. It will be darker than dark, difficult to breathe. His fear will sour the air as he waits in terror to be discovered.

As he leaves the back wall and starts along the wall on the other side, the foot of a suspended stepladder hits him in the shoulder. He jumps in fear and swears out loud. Immediately, a dog with a deep throaty growl barks just a few feet from him. Rickie turns quickly to see where the sound comes from. He is going to be attacked and torn up. How has it gotten in without his having heard it? Rickie turns around in a complete circle. No dog. Where, then? The dog barks again. It's outside, on the other side of the tall metal fence covered in bougainvillea and climbing roses which separates this property from that of the house in back! The neighbor's dog. It *is* only a few feet away, but on the other side of the fence. Thank God! Where was it yesterday? No matter. He has to be careful now before the dog lets everyone know that a prowler is around.

He runs his hand carefully over the splintery wood of the studs, follows the lines of the ladder legs, and realizes that someone has driven long nails in each stud to suspend the six-foot wooden ladder. Rickie could cry for joy. For the first time, he truly believes he has a chance. All he has to do is to take the ladder down without causing the dog to go off again, cross the yard and get it into the house without being detected.

He eases it off the wall and heads for the open doorway. Now that his eyes have become accustomed to the almost total darkness inside the garage, the yard, in spite of the shade of the avocado tree, seems cast in brilliant light. Where is it coming from? Street lights, lights at the windows of those bedding down late or rising early, and front porch and backyard lights that stay lit throughout the night. It's too bright!

He walks quickly and soundlessly across the yard under the avocado tree to the back door. He holds the ladder on his shoulder like a battering ram. The skin on his neck and back tingles with fear from the expectation that the dog will begin to bark again and someone will call out, "Stop! Drop it! Get on your knees!" He stands the ladder up and pulls the screen door open. He knows he is making too much noise in his haste to get inside, opening the screen door and scraping the ladder on the concrete step. The dog barks once, listens, and barks again. Rickie wants to turn around but he doesn't dare, fearing that he will discover someone smugly watching him with a nine millimeter pointed right at his head. He hurries into the house, the screen door banging on the side and then foot of the ladder as he drags it inside. "Oh, God," he cries out quietly, desperately; the dog begins to bark in earnest now. He drags the ladder through the house to the hallway beneath the attic access door. In a rush, he sets it up, climbs up, and pushes on the rectangular panel. It gives easily. He pushes it up and over. He hears a man yell angrily at the dog to shut up, for Chrissake, and the dog quiets.

Because the roof has a steep pitch, there is room in the middle of the attic for someone Rickie's size to actually stand. Dark cottony insulation has been blown all over the floor of the attic. It is covered with a fine dust from not having been disturbed in years. Nothing is stored here. At each end there is a louvered vent covered with a screen to prevent squirrels and rats from getting into the attic. It is hot and dusty up here, the heat of the day ticking and creaking in the rafters. Rickie's head and shoulders are through the opening. Electrical wires pass by him across the floor at eye level. He knows he must step only on the joists; if he doesn't, if he steps in the area between, he might put his foot through the plaster ceiling.

He hears noises outside. The dog has stopped barking, but he thinks he hears leaves being kicked or fallen twigs snapping beneath someone's heavy tread. He climbs all the way up into the attic and kneels on two parallel joists. He leaves the stepladder where it is. Later, he can get a hand on it and pull it up into the attic with him. For now, he slides the cover over the access door and secures it in place with a quiet thump. He listens but he hears nothing except his own breathing and pounding heart. He needs to get to one side or the other; he chooses the driveway side, partially shadowed now by the tree in the neighbor's yard. He crawls to the far side of the attic near the vent, making sure to place his hands and knees on boards, eases himself down slowly into a sitting position and listens hard. He hears nothing. Maybe he has just heard the dog moving around. Or his own fear.

There is no comfortable place to sit. Joists run across the ceiling floor with just enough space between them for him to lie down, but that will mean becoming covered with dust and dirt. He feels a sneeze coming on, and he squeezes his nose hard to prevent it. If he clears the insulation out of the way and gets low enough, it will be possible to hide from view. He will save that job for later. In the meantime, however, he sits with his back against the wall, perched on the narrow edge of a two-by-four. He tries to think of anything else but the situation at hand.

His grandfather knew about building houses, knew the names of things, sometimes even knew them in English, which he spoke with a thick accent that made Rickie laugh. But never in public. He would never hold his grandfather up for ridicule in public; he had too much respect for him. After he died, Rickie never mentioned him again, not to his friends. *Abuelo* was like some treasure, like... Rickie has nothing to compare him to since he has no possession he values in any measure similar to his grandfather. So, he simply put him away, out of sight, out of speaking, so that no stupid homie would make the mistake of joking about him.

He remembers that his grandfather would say "share" when he meant "chair"—"Sit down in your share, *mi'jo*," he would say, patting the chair at the table on his right-hand side. It was a privilege to sit next to him. "No, *abuelito*, it is chair, ch, ch, chair, not share," Rickie would say, and he and his grandfather would laugh. "*Pues, siéntate aquí, mi'jo*," he would say as he patted the chair again. "Tell me all about your day in school," he would say in Spanish. Rickie, worried that he had insulted him, would search his face, but he did not find any sign of injury there, only a true desire to hear about the little life of his grandson. Oh, God, where have those days gone? Rickie wonders, a jolt of longing and self-pity and love for his grandfather flowing through his body.

Where will he hide if they come? It is dark where the pitch of the roof meets the walls. He will get on his stomach between the joists and scootch as far back there as he can. He will lie low, bury his head. Maybe they will think he is a pile of rags or clothes. If he lies very still...

He will have to clear a space soon. He knows it will get him sneezing, so he should do it sooner than later.

This is an old house, maybe forty or fifty years old, maybe even older. His grandfather told him about the small block houses built for soldiers who had fought in the war against the Germans. Which war was that? Rickie heard teachers mention this war and that war, this event and that event, but he never cared to listen hard enough to make any of the information stick. Is this one of those houses, or had it been built earlier? His grandfather would know. How did he, a man who hadn't lived in this country even half of his life, know these things?

It's warm up here even though it's the middle of the night. What time can it be? Two, three o'clock? Not even that late? He has no idea. No matter, the roof still radiates the heat of the day, and the air, undisturbed for years, maybe decades, is redolent with the scent of baked dust and timber. It isn't an unpleasant smell. It is somehow reminiscent of old people in general, his grandfather in particular. He wishes, can almost make himself believe, that his grandfather is still alive, that he might walk out of this place and go home and find him there once more.

Go home. He is never going to go home. A terrible panic and sadness well up in the pit of his stomach. Maybe he should get out of here and run, run to his father in Ventura. He should get up and run toward the ocean—he knows which direction that is—run until he collapses, rest for a few minutes, and run again until he finds the sand and the water. How far is it? Twenty, thirty miles? He can do it. Once he finds the beach, he will run along the sand until he comes to Ventura and then... What? Finds his father? What is he *thinking*? His father never wanted him before; what makes him think he'll want him now, particularly after he hears what Rickie has done? No way! He shakes his head in disgust at the thought of his father and at his own crazy thinking, and adjusts his sitting position.

Tension has built up in his legs with the thought of getting up and running, but now it begins to lessen. The whole neighborhood is crawling with cops. They probably have the dogs out as well. The idea of running out the front door into a waiting army of cops with their Berettas or Glocks drawn, who will feel no hesitation at gunning down a cop killer; the image of himself being chased down by German Shepherds or dead-eyed Dobermans and finally being overtaken and torn apart—both of these pictures root him in place.

Maybe he will be one of the lucky ones, someone who gets away. No, that's impossible. They already have Alex. Of course they will connect the two of them. Rickie's prints are all over the cop's gun. Oh, Jesus, he is going to die.

He sits with his back against the dry and splintery wood, perched uncomfortably on a two-by-four, his arms around his drawn-up knees where he rests his head. He wants to cry, but the tears will not come. What will his grandmother think? His coach? His brother and sister? They won't understand. They'll be shocked. He can see them shaking their heads in sadness and disbelief, each of them asking how Rickie could have become a cop killer and why hadn't they seen it coming. They won't have any answers. *He* doesn't know himself. Things just happened, as though behind some kind of curtain. He remembers leaving his house—why? What made him leave? He met Alex. Then the electronics store, beating on the door. And then the cops and running and then the young cop and the scar on his face and then nothing, nothing but a sort of redness, a red drapery before his eyes, until the pistol fires and the cop falls with that look in his eyes, so young, so surprised, so sad; it's like looking into the eyes of one of his friends.

He wants to think of something else. School. Tomorrow, no, today by now, will be a school day. Will people know by the time school starts? Will Claudia know? Dennis? Tony? Oscar? He thinks with joyless pride for a brief moment that he has shown that dumbass. Let him top this! Will people cry? Will someone tag "RIP Grt Whyte"? Will people buy black T-shirts and have R.I.P. scripted on the back as they do when others die? But who really knows him or cares about him enough? Claudia will cry. She will be sad because she is a sweet girl, maybe even more because she will feel guilty about what went on at the wedding reception. She will cry maybe because she loves him, but he also knows that she will make sure it is in public in order to draw the most attention and sympathy. Girlfriends and girls who don't even know her will come to her and put an arm around her or hug her and share the limelight.

The tears well up in his eyes for himself as he imagines other people's sadness, but also as he realizes that not many will care. He has been so successful in making himself a shadow in the hallways that people either fear him or don't know him. Phelan. Phelan will be sad. But Phelan cares for all of them, all of his students, Rickie among them, and in its being generalized, the caring is somehow on the surface, not very deep. Yes, Phelan will be genuinely sorry, but other kids, other issues, will command his attention. And next year there will be a whole new crop of students for the teacher to care about and try to teach. Who will *really* miss him, and not for just a few days? His grandmother, maybe Daisy and Bill for a while. Bill and Daisy will be hurt, even angry with him. But his grandmother—she will feel his loss deep within her. She won't think of him as he is now; she will remember the little boy she and his grandfather rescued from selfish, indifferent parents. He knows that even after she returns to Mexico to live with her sister, her heart will ache for her lost grandchild.

Suddenly, he feels that ache himself, and tears spill out of his eyes. He feels very young, strange inside his teenage body.

He needs to think of something else, something that will not make him sad. He does as teachers do—he assigns himself a topic. Favorite TV shows. He goes through a list of the sitcoms that come on in the late afternoon and early evening, all involving cute white or black girls, and a guy girls find cute and his stupid friend. What about them? He doesn't watch them for longer than a minute, so he can't remember anything specific about them. The characters blend in with the people in the commercials for fast foods, cereal, candy and toys that interrupt the story. For all the color and flashiness and noise, there is a blandness about it all that makes all of it difficult to remember.

He thinks of *The Simpsons* and *South Park*, two shows he hardly ever misses. The kids are wise and the adults befuddled and corruptible. Someone finally made TV shows about what kids suspect—adults don't have much wisdom or many values. They make it up as they go along and only *tell* kids that they believe this or that.

But once again, he can't remember any particular episode with clarity. Is it because of the amount of marijuana he's been smoking? He begins to feel desperation that he can't remember anything. He tries to see some image, some person or place by pressing his eyes shut, but all he sees is a sheet of black and then red and then little floating things like spiky balls.

He opens his eyes again. It feels like everything is a lie, everyone a liar, nothing what it seems. His coach and some of his teachers, only a few really, are the only adults he partially trusts, but he doesn't really know them and they don't know him.

What *about* his teachers? He remembers one time his team played in a tournament in one of the towns in the foothills, not far away in terms of mileage, but light years away in other respects. The hillside houses were shaded by big leafy trees, yards were cool and verdant and neatly trimmed, the people all Anglo and driving SUV's or Mercedes, Audis or Lexuses. The high school where they played was clean and untouched by graffiti.

After the game, they stopped at a big supermarket to buy drinks and chips. It was clean and bright, the floors polished and the aisles wide, not like the market where his grandmother shops where only one person at a time can push a cart down an aisle, and so most people don't, opting to carry things in small hand baskets or juggle them in their arms.

Rickie had been studying the magazines displayed at the end of an aisle in this large supermarket. When he turned to head for the front of the store, he almost bumped into his history teacher, Mrs. Halprin.

"Rickie," she said, not hiding the surprise and the fact that it was not totally pleasant behind the smile frozen on her face, "what are you doing here?"

Suddenly it seemed too bright and polished in there, the music—the Beach Boys singing "I wish they all could be California girls..."—too loud. Rickie felt like a trespasser. "My team... tournament at the high school," he stammered.

Coach Vega turned the corner of the aisle, saw them talking, and came along quickly. Rickie could read the fear on his face that something bad had happened, that Rickie had said something or been caught stealing. After they had introduced themselves and it had been established that there was nothing wrong, Mrs. Halprin—she had always insisted on being called "Missus"—and Coach Vega stood in the aisle and talked in quiet voices, she in jeans and a sweatshirt, he handsome in his baseball uniform. She was obviously impressed with his lean good looks and self-conscious about being caught in casual clothes.

"She don't have her armor on," Lenny had whispered to Rickie after Coach told him to rejoin his teammates; the team gathered at the far end of the aisle. Lenny and Rickie had Mrs. Halprin for U.S. History this year.

"Huh?"

"Her armor, her school clothes. You know, those old lady teacher clothes. She'd be almost pretty if she didn't have that stick up her ass. How old you think she is?"

The members of the team watched their coach and the teacher converse. They could see that Mrs. Halprin was uncomfortable being the one observed.

"I don't know. Old. Why is her hair like a helmet?"

"I wonder if she is telling him about one of her wonderful kids or her important husband. Man, I am so sick of hearing about them."

Mrs. Halprin nodded eagerly and made slight turning motions to signal that she wanted to get away. Coach let her. He held out his hand, and she shook it. Lenny called good-bye to her. The others waved.

What will she think about Rickie? Of course, her opinion of

him will be confirmed; she always looked at him like he was a dangerous alien, not a member of the same species as her. And when she talked about the poor neighborhoods around the school, it was with distaste and wariness and obvious relief that this wasn't her reality. He can imagine her tomorrow morning at the front of the room pausing dramatically for a second after she has said that tragedy in places like this is inevitable, you must go to college and get away, make a better life... And then she'll proceed with the lesson. Her worksheets on the Gilded Age in the U.S. or her lecture notes on Theodore Roosevelt are of great importance. We have to get through the Great Depression before the school year ends.

Coach Vega is the person Rickie trusts the most. If Rickie only knew exactly where he lived, he'd chance it. He'd leave this place, run without stopping until he found him, fall into his arms—yes, he would throw his arms around him—and beg for protection. But with agonizing frustration, he is forced to accept the fact again that he has no idea where Coach lives.

He turns his attention to the night outside. He hears something and strains to make it out. No voice, no footsteps, but something. He pushes himself up carefully and stands. His legs ache; his rear end is sore from sitting on the edge of the board. He stands so that he's closer to the screened vent and looks out. The vent is still a couple of feet above him, so all he can see is the top of the tree. It is tossing side to side. The air moves in the attic. The winds have returned. They will blow the smog and heat away. Tomorrow will be cooler and clearer, not so oppressive. He'll feel better tomorrow.

And then with a certainty that weakens his knees and makes him sit again, he realizes again that there will be no tomorrow.

They are out there, somewhere, on the sidewalks, in back yards, on the streets, with spotlights and long flashlights and dogs, moving relentlessly and grimly from block to block through the neighborhood, drawing closer and closer. Sometime in the night they will find him, and they will need no excuse to kill him. He sobs, terrified at the picture he sees in his mind of the execution he knows is coming.

Unless the guy didn't die. Maybe he lived. Maybe Rickie imagined the picture he had of the back of the cop's head exploding and blood and bone and brain spitting forth from the wound. Maybe the bullet only grazed the side of his head.

No, he knows too well that the picture is real. There is another hope, however.

Maybe there can be some kind of miraculous intervention, God or the Virgin Mary or Jesus or an angel stepping between him and the police, throwing a cloak of obscurity over him. He has heard people talk about miraculous events on TV, when an angel protected them from being killed in a shootout or a car wreck, or Jesus or the Madonna had appeared to them and cured them of cancer. Why? Why would they do that? How did a person get that to happen? He knows so little about religious things. He used to attend Mass with his grandmother, but she said it was not the same. She missed *La Virgencita*, she said; they must hope that She, along with *San Judas* and *Jesucristo*, still looked after their children even here in this country. She lights candles for them and places them on a table in the living room.

Rickie hadn't understood. He remembered that there was a statue of the Madonna at the front of the church, and once, as a little boy, he pointed Her out to his grandmother with the hope that she hadn't seen the statue before and, once she did, she would be comforted. His grandmother said she had seen this pretty white Virgin; she said he would understand better when they went to Mexico and Mexico became part of his blood. Then she had looked at him for a long moment and sighed.

He doesn't want mournful thoughts. He forces himself to turn back to the possibility of divine intervention. Why do some people get angels to help them or Jesus to put his hand on them and cure them? Is it like the lottery, just blind luck, or do they have to do something to deserve it? What has he done? He has been over this territory before and has not been successful in finding anything in his life to warrant salvation. He has been a good baseball player, but he knows that his talent was given to him. He has taken it for granted, never thanked God for his sure glove hand, his graceful agility, or his keen eye at the plate. He has heard award recipients on TV thank Jesus for their success, but it always sounded dishonest to him.

Should Rickie have thanked God before each game, taken a knee along the first base line and bowed his head in prayer before each game? Wouldn't God know it was phony? And, anyway, he has grown tired of baseball and in a year or even after this season, he's going to quit. So he's already throwing away his gift. He has... He can't think of anything, so he settles on the fact that he's still a kid. Kids make mistakes, they have to make mistakes in order to learn, isn't that what everybody says? He has a right to have this mistake forgiven. He deserves it.

His thoughts grow wilder and more desperate as he tries to find a strong reason why he shouldn't die. He sits perched on the board again, his arms around his knees drawn up to his chin and his face resting on his knees, and he goes over and over the same people and places and events, searching for a reason why he should be allowed to continue to live. He knows that once he thinks of it, he will be okay, he won't die.

He sits this way for another half-hour until he begins to doze. He wants to lie down. With his feet he pushes away the insulation from between two of the joists, covering his mouth and nose with his T-shirt to keep the dust out. When the dust has settled, he stretches out in the space between and rests his head on his crossed arms. He remembers that he should pull the ladder up, but he is too sleepy. He'll get it when he wakes up. He falls into uneasy sleep, his ears straining to hear any noise that might signal that the cops have finally found him.

CHAPTER 21

By this time the police know everything, of course, everything but where Rickie is. Alex tells them all they need to know, but not about the house.

"You're going down for murdering a cop, you punkass motherfucker!" a cop yells at him at the station, but Alex barely understands the words or registers the pain in his arms and hands restrained behind his back or anything else. He barely knows where he is.

He tells the story at the station in painful stops and starts. Of going to the electronics store with the idea of doing some damage because the owner had treated them like shit; of beating on the door with a pry bar, setting off the alarm and running through the neighborhood; of seeing the cop car and splitting up; of his trying to hide behind some low bushes next to an apartment building but being found and giving up; of sitting in the cop car and hearing the weapon discharge; and of coming on to the scene and watching in horror as the young cop slumped to the ground. Alex was stunned by the ordinariness of that, the surprise and hurt on the face draining to no expression at all. Lifelessness, the look of death and nothingness, impressed itself on his memory and terrified him. He didn't see a serene first glimpse of the afterlife on the young officer's face. No, just life become not life, a human being become a body.

The image haunts him as he sits in cuffs in the back seat of the cop car on the way to the station, and during the booking process when he sits on a hard blue plastic chair.

The sirens and lights and pounding on the door waken Berta. When she opens it, four heavily armed police in riot gear brush by her with rifles pointed and yelling something in anger and fear that she doesn't understand. Another one rushes her out of the house and stands in front of her and demands Rickie, something about Rickie, something about a policeman. She repeats over and over, "*No entiendo. Dime...no entiendo. Ay, Dios mío,*" she says, making the sign of the Cross, "*Tengo que llamarle por teléfono a mi'jo.*" She stands in the yard in her old nightgown, ashamed to be outside like this, patting her hair distractedly, waiting for a Spanish-speaking officer. She reaches for her Rosary in her apron pocket, but, of course, she is not wearing her apron this time of night; the Rosary is on her dresser. Two officers lead her back inside when they are sure that Rickie is not there. They allow her to get her robe and her Rosary from her bedroom; she finds the paper Ricardo has written his number on.

"I don't know," she says after Ricardo finally answers. "They say too many things so fast. They yell at me, Ricardo, like I have done something wrong. I do not understand. It is something about Junior shooting a policeman."

"Oh, Jesus," he says. "Let me talk to them, 'Amá," he says to her.

"Please. Explain my son," she asks in English and hands the officer the phone.

She watches as the officer speaks to Ricardo in English, but she cannot understand, particularly when the officer catches her watching him and turns away from her. When he is finished speaking, the officer motions for her to sit on the couch. Then he gives her the phone. He stands above her as she hears what has taken place, but she makes no outburst. She just stares blankly, shaking her head slightly, as though looking into the heart of a vastly larger unknown.

"Do you understand, 'Amá?" Ricardo asks. She nods her head that she does, but does not speak. "Are you all right? I'll call Bill and Daisy to come be with you. I'm coming down right now. I'll be there soon."

Bill and Daisy are there within half an hour. Daisy sits with her grandmother and pats her hand. Bill talks quietly with the police. He watches as they pick through and examine Rickie's belongings.

Later, her son and grandchildren sit with Berta in vigil. They don't speak. Daisy sits next to her grandmother on the sofa. Ricardo gets a chair from the kitchen and sits across from her. Bill perches on the arm of the sofa, not looking at or speaking to his father. They all stare at their thoughts and wait for the inevitable call or knock on the door or, worse, the burst of gunfire.

Out in the neighborhood the search continues. The low-flying helicopters rattle and boom in circles with bright searchlights probing empty lots and backyards. Patrol cars rush up and down streets with sirens crying. Someone thinks the kid has been spotted near the middle school. Anyone unlucky enough to be out on the streets is detained and questioned roughly.

Grim determination spreads deep into the neighborhood like the rivers of rainwater that flow on the streets and gather in small lakes at intersections during wet winters. This killer isn't going to get away.

Dogs strain at leashes, up alleys and through yards, glad to be out of their kennels. They pick up the scent and the excitement. Cops cluster at various checkpoints. Occasionally a siren whoops and a patrol car speeds off down Landerman or some side street.

Rickie wakes suddenly from a tortured sleep in which strange and shadowy beings run into and out of houses, some in terror, others in relentless and hulking pursuit, seeking bloody vengeance. He lifts his head and listens. Feet tread on the leaves that blanket the yard from the previous fall. The police. They know he is here. They whisper, call softly to dogs that pull their handlers forward. With fear gripping and choking him, he hears footsteps on the driveway, a boot crunching the glass from the broken window, a whispered curse, and then Rickie hears the screen door open.

He flattens himself as best he can, knowing it will not be enough. And then he remembers that he has not dragged the stepladder up with him. Only moments are left. What should he say? What can he do? His chest begins to heave in fear. He can hear them below now. The ladder scrapes on the floor, dog nails click and scrabble on the hard wood, and men whisper commands to one another. Rickie's eyes are fixed on the hatch. He knows it will rise up, a hand with a weapon in it will precede a head with fearful, angry eyes.

"Don't shoot!" he cries out. "I'm up here. Don't shoot, please," he adds. "I'm sorry."

The cover bursts away to the side. A hand and a weapon and a helmeted head emerge from below.

"Put your hands where I can see them, you fuck. Now!"

"Don't shoot, please. My arms are asleep. I can't feel them."

More of the torso emerges. The weapon and the light are extended closer to Rickie's forehead. "Move! Let me see your hands."

His head has been on his crossed arms. He opens and closes his hands, desperately trying to get the blood flowing again.

"You can see my hands. I don't have nothing. You can see them," he cries.

"Don't tell me what I can see! Get them away from your body!"

Rickie rises up on his chest, lifting his head, hoping to be able to free an arm. He rises up on one elbow.

"Get down, kid. Get down and put your hands out where I can see them. Do it! Slowly!"

Rickie flattens himself again. It is then that his left arm betrays him. It jerks out quickly in front of him.

"No!" he cries out as he sees fear charge the officer's eyes and the brilliant flash of light, and he hears the deafening explosion for a brief instant before light and sound and memory and life itself are scattered into the night.

And in that instant, before the bullet slams through fragile bone and explodes the soft mass behind, Rickie knows what has been bearing down on him, what threatened to run him over. It has been there his whole life; he has known it all along. Finally, it has arrived. There will be peace now. What has threatened has finally come to pass. He can relax. He has nothing to prove, nothing to be strong against. He is free and untouchable. He can be a boy again. He can laugh and cry, hold his grandfather's rough hand and look into his eyes. They can walk together again as they had done when his grandfather discovered him asleep in the shed, and Rickie will know he is safe. He can walk with his grandmother, a little boy holding her hand and jumping in the puddles as they walk home together from school. No more worries. No more hurt, no more pain. Nothing.

CHAPTER 22

"Y ou all right? What's going on?" a voice calls from below.

"Got him! Got his ass! He was going for a weapon," the officer yells.

"Come down, Becker, " a voice calls. "I want to take a look before the others get here."

Becker recognizes the voice. The owner of it had been right behind his partner and him on the way into the house.

The only officers in the house now are members of L.A.'s elite anti-gang unit. The K-9 officers have taken the dogs outside.

Ever since its inception, the unit has been given free reign. Supervisors turn a blind eye to its questionable practices; formal inquiries, the few times they are made, are always *pro forma* and without any disciplinary consequences. Everything justifies bringing L.A.'s burgeoning gang violence under control. Few people ask questions.

Becker climbs down the ladder and his fellow officer brushes by him on the way up.

They all jump when another shot rings out.

"What the hell?"

"What's going on?"

"He went for his weapon again," the man on the ladder calls out.

"My turn," a third officer says. "I think I know this punk." He climbs up the ladder after the second officer comes down.

"I knew this little creep," he calls from above. His large form blocks most of the entrance to the attic and muffles his voice. "He tags "Great White" or some such shit, like he's a vicious shark. Well, R.I.P. Great White, you little fucker. Tag *this!*"

The shot rings out just before a number of other patrol cars pull up.

"C'mon down. We're done."

Becker finally steps outside the abandoned house when the body is wheeled into the coroner's van. He wonders momentarily about the house, who had lived there, where they had gone. A sea of nameless brown faces populates these neighborhoods now; the people are all the same to him, unknown and interchangeable. He knows that they don't stay long if they can afford to move elsewhere.

He looks at the facade of the house with its pagoda roof and shutters suggestive of Chinese characters, and he shakes his head at the irony of its history. The poor bastard who built it back in, what, 1910? The 1920s?—pleased to have a new house in the current style, a comfortable bungalow not far from Hollywood—what had happened to him and his family? They could never have envisioned this. What happened to the ones who have lived here since?

Becker shrugs his shoulders and looks up at the night sky expecting to see the approach of dawn, an increase of light in back of the mountains, but there is none. It is still the dead of night. Birds have begun to chatter in the trees, however, because the peaceful night has erupted in noise and bright light. The breeze continues to cool the air and rustle the leaves.

There will be a party at the apartment in Van Nuys that the members of the anti-gang unit keep secretly for themselves. After they take down a gangster or make a big bust, the officers gather at the apartment to celebrate. Tonight it will be subdued because of the dead officer, but Becker will be the center of attention. He'll have to recount how he and his partner were right in back of the K-9 unit and found the ladder in the hallway; how he knew the situation right then and jumped on the ladder, pushed open the hatch, saw the kid's arm move, and placed a shot dead center, right above the bridge of the nose. He'll be high-fived and slapped on the back.

Becker finds his partner waiting for him at the car.

"Are we headed for Van Nuys?" his partner asks as they get in.

"Yeah, why not?"

"You think it's okay? I mean, considering…?"

"We'll be at the officer's funeral. Did you know him?"

"No. He was a rookie. I didn't know him."

"Me neither. Let it go. Get in. We'll just have a couple of beers."

CHAPTER 23

n a few hours, the sky in the east begins to lighten. The neighborhood awakens and goes to work. Women wait for buses to take them to the houses south of Ventura Boulevard, or to Beverly Hills, Bel Air, and Brentwood. Men go off to their jobs at Home Depot or Sears or Costco as assistant managers, cashiers, salesmen, or warehousemen, or as truck drivers, or to street corners in search of a day's labor. Others check mowers and gardening tools in the beds of their pickups. Commercial airliners and private jets begin to roar out of the airport before the sky is fully lighted.

In another hour, as the school children begin to make their reluctant way out front doors, the story of the young cop who has been killed and of the boy who shot him and been killed himself, makes its way in quiet voices throughout the neighborhood. Everyone is incredulous at first. It doesn't make sense. No one understands why a kid who was such a good baseball player would kill a good young cop, one of our own, maybe even from this neighborhood. Why does it happen? It's the parents, they say. What was the kid doing out so late on a Sunday night, a school night? It's the schools. It's video games that make death look so easy and unreal, and music groups that record so-called songs about killing and suicide. It's the neighborhood itself. It's a combination of everything. It's the times we live in, they say, and shake their heads at this latest horrible thing to happen.

The Deans at the high school quickly put in a call for grief counselors to come to the school, and they, along with others, sit through the day in circles of teenagers who stumble through a sentence or two and then fall silent. The number of kids who come to the empty classrooms to grieve surprises Wagner. Throughout the day, some adults who knew Rickie gather in the lunchroom and say in lowered voices that he was incorrigible, that this or something like it was bound to happen. Some, like Bill Phelan and a few other teachers and counselors, join the grieving teenagers and wonder if they could have done more for the boy. They speak in hushed tones about the good they saw in Rickie. Phelan recalls the assurance Rickie gave him of getting an 'A' in his class; Lopez says that Rickie was troubled and had started out in life as a little boy with the same hopes and dreams as anyone else. Maltrey is quiet, saying nothing about the incident of the previous Friday, just three days before. He sits with the others in mournful silence.

During the week Dennis and Tony, swollen-eyed and mournful, carry shoeboxes with a slot cut in the top and decorated with Rickie's photo and "R.I.P. Rickie" and "We miss you, Rickie" written on them. Oscar joins them sometimes. They go from classroom to classroom, where teachers and students reach into pockets and pull out dollars and stuff them into the boxes. The secretaries and custodians and cafeteria people contribute, too. Their generosity is real and uncalculated; they know the money is for Rickie's burial. No one blames the grandmother. People know that even a simple funeral is expensive, and the school is one of the few resources to turn to.

At the morning break and again at lunch, the boys stand on the steps leading to the auditorium. They hold a larger photo of the dead boy and collect money. Claudia stands with them in quiet gloom. Others join them; many wear baseball hats or black T-shirts with Rickie's photo and "R.I.P. Rickie" printed on them, produced by a storefront business in the neighborhood that has experience doing this sort of thing on short notice. Other students scrawl R.I.P. on their shirts with anything that will show—marker, lipstick, even liquid whiteout. All of the students stand in gloomy groups of two or three or more. During the first few days, there is no laughter, no shouting across the quad before the bell rings. When the bell does ring to end the morning break or lunch, the students move slowly and quietly to class.

Throughout the week, the local TV stations and the *Times* and the *Daily News* run segments or print articles about the rookie cop and his family, his hopes and aspirations, and the fact that he had a good heart. They write, too, about the frightening growth of gangs in Los Angeles.

Reporters wait outside Berta's house to interview members of the family. Ricardo refuses to speak. Bill is angry—"Three shots to the face? At close range? That's execution. There was no need for that." Daisy brushes by the press of reporters and news cameras on the way into the house. She stops at the doorway and turns to face the gathering. "I don't have anything to say about it except how sad and angry I am. I just lost a brother, his face all shot up on purpose, just another Mexican shot dead. The policeman's family lost a son and a brother, a husband and a father. He shouldn't have died. My brother either. What do you want me to say? It's a needless tragedy. Maybe you should figure out why these things happen and how to stop them rather than wasting your time here. You think we have the answers? His grandmother? We don't."

The local TV stations carry the funeral of the fallen officer and re-play it on the evening news. The mayor and the Chief both speak of the young man's desire to serve the community; the camera pans often to the officer's tearful wife holding their daughter. Neither newspaper mentions Rickie's funeral, though a reporter from the *Daily News* attends for a while and is surprised and disgusted by the number of people in attendance and the out-pouring of grief for a cop-killer. He writes a short piece on the service that's cut out of respect for Officer Padilla.

The championship game is cancelled. Coach Vega shows up at Rickie's service, but he leaves hurriedly before anyone can speak with him. He is too conflicted to speak to the media.

The man with the red hair comes forward. "I could almost swear he didn't have a weapon in his hand. Yeah, I read that the reason they had to shoot him so many times was that he kept threatening them with Officer Padilla's weapon. I remember the kid's hands being empty. But everything happened so fast, I could have missed it. Mostly I remember his face, wild-eyed and scared, like a horse in a stable fire. I thought gangsters were chasing him. I didn't know. He looked so young and scared. I can't imagine him killing anyone, a cop particularly."

CHAPTER 24

Early the next week, Berta is washing the morning dishes when she hears a knock on the security door, but she doesn't respond. The front door is open, but she keeps the security door locked now. She's safe. Maybe she imagined the knock. She has been standing at the sink looking out onto the backyard but not truly seeing. Each morning she rises and hopes that she imagined everything. Any minute, she expects to hear Junior open his door and head for the bathroom, and she will be able to relax, even smile, at this. Order will be re-established. Life will go on, hope will blossom again.

There is another knock on the security door, this time definite and louder. Perhaps it is more reporters. Why now? She goes to the living room and leaning over, peers out the door without being seen. Three boys stand nervously foot-to-foot at the bottom of the steps, each holding a shoebox and looking down at his feet. She does not recognize any one of them.

"*Señora,*" Tony says quietly when Berta comes to the door. "*Colectamos este dinero para usted.*" He doesn't look up.

"*Para* Rickie's funeral," Dennis says.

"*Sí,* Rickie's funeral," Tony says.

They remove the tops of the shoeboxes, carefully peeling back the tape that secures top to bottom, and proudly hold them out to her. Each box is filled with crumpled dollar bills. She opens the door, takes the boxes, and cradles them in her arms.

"Many thanks," she says, and no one speaks for a moment. "Where is the boy that sometimes came here? *Alejandro?*"

"Alex? He was with Rickie that night. They got him," Oscar says.

"Is he...?"

"No, *Señora.* The cops arrested him. He's in Juvy... Juvenile Hall... jail...right now."

She shakes her head sadly. "I haven't seen you boys before," she says in Spanish. She looks at them and speaks slowly. They speak a rough mix of Spanish and English; she doesn't know how well they understand.

"Would you like to come in? See Junior's...Rickie's room?"

The boys look from one to another, unsure what to do. "You can see his trophies," she says and opens the door wider to let them in.

They file in slowly and enter the bedroom. Berta has moved the votive candles from the little table in the living room where they have stood for years to a central place on Junior's dresser, surrounded by his trophies and other baseball artifacts. *San Judas Tadeo* is here—the saint who cares for everyone, good and bad, and who listens even when the cause has been lost. Berta asks him to make Junior's death the last one. No more death. No more heartache, please. Of course, *La Virgencita* and *Jesucristo* are here as well. The brightly colored glasses holding new candles have been washed and polished, and the low flames burn steadily, filling the room with the sanctified smell of candle wax.

Berta closes the boxes and lines them up neatly on Junior's pillow, and then sits at the foot of the bed facing the crowded dresser, a place she has sat often during the past days. The boys stand in front of the dresser and look, their backs to her. Oscar picks up a trophy. Dennis and Tony look back at her to make sure it's all right.

"Go ahead, look," Berta says. "You can hold them. They won't break."

"He had *a lot* of trophies," Tony says, shaking his head in amazement. Oscar looks at him and back at the trophy and replaces it.

"Yeah. Everyone said he was real good," Dennis says. Tony nods in agreement. "He should've played at school, but him and Alex got caught... You know, the car." He glances at Rickie's grandmother. She sits quietly, fingering the beads of her Rosary.

"Was Junior your friend?" she asks. The boys turn to her. They look at one another. Tony and Dennis nod their heads yes.

"Did you go to school with him for many years?"

Dennis raises his hand. "Him and me did," indicating Tony. "I remember he loved his grandpa. Alex and him and me and Tony had the same teachers in elementary. I remember you. Waiting for him on the sidewalk across the street."

"He was a good boy. Happy then." Her eyes have begun to glisten. The boys nod. No one speaks.

"Maybe he is happy now," she says softly.

"Sí, *Señora*." Tears leak down Tony's cheeks, which he wipes away with the palm of his hand.

"I don't know why he did what he did. Do you know?" she says after a while. They shake their heads. The beads click softly.

"He had all his life ahead of him," she says. "You do, too. Your mothers want you to do good and be happy. That's why they work so hard. Your fathers, too. Stay in school and work hard. Be good boys. Become good men, responsible," she says, but she can see that the boys are growing restive, shifting their weight from one foot to the other and glancing toward the doorway. She knows their *abuelitas* and *tías* have given them the same message, probably over and over.

"Remember what I say," she says as she stands. "Do good now and grow to be good men." They nod as she escorts them to the front door. "Thank you for your kindness. I am happy Junior had good friends like you."

One after the other, they shake her hand and mumble goodbye and shuffle off. She watches them go down the sidewalk; when they think they are far enough away, they break into a run, elbowing each other and laughing, like students released from school.

Berta pulls the security door closed and goes back into Junior's bedroom. She looks around the room before she smooths the spread and leaves. She ignores the shoeboxes.

It is as though the shot that killed the policeman and the shots that killed Junior have blown a hole in this house. It is too empty, too silent, suddenly too big. She goes from room to room—the living room silent now with the TV off, the dining room with unopened mail and circulars spilled onto the table, her bedroom and bathroom, the kitchen. She stands at the kitchen door and looks out on the backyard and thinks of Ricardo.

He has gone back to Ventura with the promise to return home soon. He will move into the garage until he finds a job down here, and then they will decide. At first she was doubtful about his returning home, but not now—maybe he will fill the emptiness. And maybe he will grow to be a good man himself now that he has lost this son he barely knew; maybe he will work to re-establish his relationship with Bill and Daisy, and take responsibility as a man and a father.

Bill and Daisy have returned to work and school, but they come by often in the evenings to check on her, and she is happy. They bring her food and sit with her in the living room, watch TV without speaking, each absorbed in thought. Berta hopes Bill will listen to her about forgiving his father now that he, too, has seen how fragile life is and how quickly it can be taken.

She wonders if the day will ever come when she will join her sister in Mexico. She remembers telling Junior on the night of the shooting that she was going to move soon and how upset he was. Somehow, with his death, the happiness she envisioned seems farther away, maybe impossible—how will she escape this sadness?

She stopped understanding the boy when he became a teenager, when he became so intense and so quick to anger; she stopped being able to reach him when he withdrew so far into himself and hardly spoke with her. In order to remember and love Junior easily and freely again, she has to separate the boy who died from the little boy she walked to school and from the boy who went along on trips to the hardware stores and lumberyards so happily with his grandfather. She has almost forgotten that child.

When she is home from work and alone, Berta goes often into Junior's room, re-lights the candles, and sits at the end of the bed to look at the trophies and hats and other reminders of his years playing baseball, hoping that being in the presence of his things will bring her close again to her grandchild. She prays.

She dusts often, believing that these things were important to Junior and that he would be happy to see them clean and shiny.

A couple of reporters, a man and a woman, show up a few days later and ask to come inside Berta's house. They crowd into Rickie's bedroom. It's as though they believe there is an explanation somewhere that others haven't uncovered which will clarify everything. When she is asked the same questions again that she has answered all the previous week, she can only say she doesn't understand how this could have happened and how sorry she is for the policeman's family. They photograph her sitting in mournful confusion at the foot of the boy's bed with the dresser full of baseball trophies and candles mirrored in the background. She gestures hopelessly at the dresser, opens her mouth to say something, but does not. Her hand falls back to her lap and the Rosary she holds there.

Finally, she says, "He made cookies that night. Is that the way of a bad boy?"

The events of this night seep into the sad landscape of the neighborhood and are absorbed and forgotten, unless someone mentions the good young cop who was killed or the killer who played baseball so well. Other deaths take the place of these, other disappointments, other losses, and other grief. Families move out and are replaced by people who have no memory of this night. The house where Rickie hid and where he died is bulldozed the following year.

Fellow students who wore "R.I.P. Grt Whyt" or "R.I.P. Rickie" scripted in white on black T-shirts or hats soon put them away. They move through high school onto other things. Every so often, they will come across the shirt in a drawer or the hat on a clos-et shelf. Some will have trouble remembering clearly whom this particular shirt or hat was for because others will have died in the meantime. Some will get rid of it when they come across it, as though to expunge all memory of those days. And some will refold the shirt and place it neatly in the back of a drawer or place the hat deep on a shelf. They will make a point of not looking at it, content to let its importance fade into obscurity, willing to accept it as a memento of bittersweet days gone by that they haven't the time or desire to recall.

ABOUT THE AUTHOR

NICHOLAS BRADLEY worked as an English and ESL teacher in junior high, middle, and high school in Los Angeles throughout his thirty year career. The schools where he taught were in neighborhoods of poverty and crime, gangs, drugs and graffiti that formed the setting *Rickie Trujillo.* Many of the students he taught and tutored during his career were, like Rickie, active gang members and/or taggers.

During the ten years in Los Angeles preceding his teaching career, Bradley worked as a road musician, truck driver, messenger, and pianist.

He has published fiction in the *Red Cedar Review* and conducted feature interviews with jazz and classical great musicians such as Med Flory, Pete Christlieb, Tommy Newsome, Glen Johnston, and Leo Potts, all of which were published in the *Saxophone Journal.* He has also been recognized in national writing contests for two of his short stories.